Aloha Island

The Story of the Stones

by

Frank South

> *Based on concepts and characters developed by Michael Furuya, Mark Loughridge, Lisa Matsumoto, and Frank and Margaret South.*

Cover art and design, and Aloha Island map by Michael Furuya.

† The four classic word riddles adapted for *Aloha Island* are not the author's. They can be found in various forms in multiple educational books and informational websites such as: wiki.answers.com and braingle.com.

Copyright © 2012 by Aloha Island Inc.
All rights reserved.
www.thealohaislandinc.com

Published by
Deep South Publishing
205 Hunters Ridge Road
Warner Robins, Georgia 31093
www.facebook.com/DeepSouthPublishing

No part of this publication may be reproduced, stored in a retrieval system, or transmitted in any form or by any means, without the written prior permission of the copyright holder, Aloha Island Inc. Contact Aloha Island Inc. at info@thealohaislandinc.com or through the publisher.

Deep South Publishing

ISBN:0-615-68525-0
ISBN-13: 978-0-615-68525-0

For Lisa Matsumoto

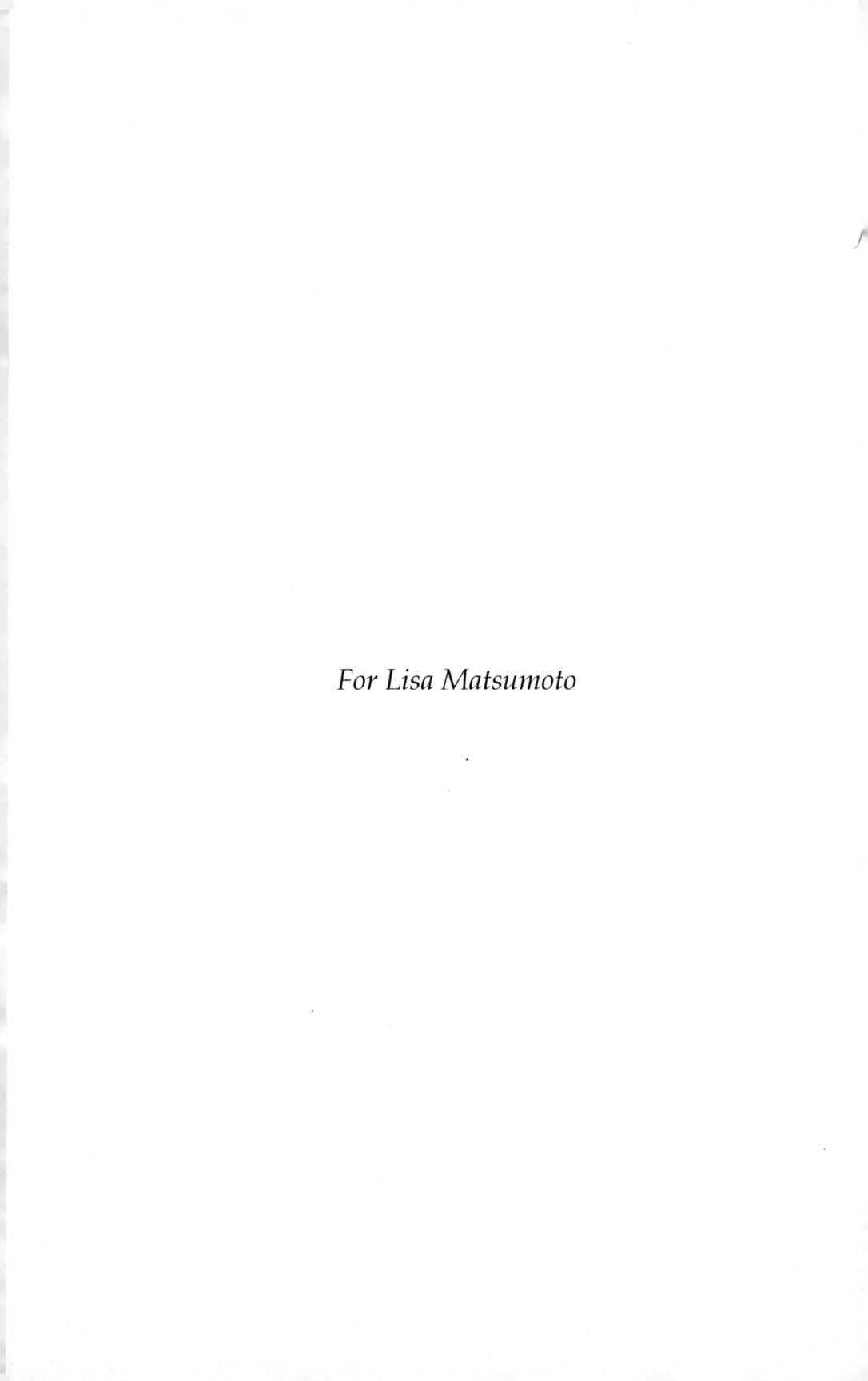

Contents

Acknowledgments vii

Map of Aloha Island viii

Chapter 1 *Ambush* 9

Chapter 2 *Escape* 15

Chapter 3 *The Bubble Bursts* 19

Chapter 4 *Biggie Brings It* 22

Chapter 5 *The Letter Drop* 25

Chapter 6 *Trouble Right Off the Bat* 27

Chapter 7 *Someone's in the Kitchen* 30

Chapter 8 *You Want Us to WHAT?* 36

Chapter 9 *Tempest in a Tide Pool* 39

Chapter 10 *The Dark Atoll* 42

Chapter 11 *The Flaming Illiterates Sneak Up* 46

Chapter 12 *A Watery Grave* 50

Chapter 13 *The Too Far Safari* 54

Chapter 14 *Fear Is Here* 57

Chapter 15 *The Story of the Stones Part 1: The Spirits' Gifts* 60

Chapter 16 *Luau Lunacy* 66

Chapter 17 *Few Chew Noodle Stew* 71

Chapter 18 *The Story of the Stones Part 2: Ignorance Attacks* 76

Chapter 19 *Morning Madness* 81

Chapter 20 *Prisoner of the Dark Atoll* 85

Chapter 21 *Prime Minister Rule* 90

Chapter 22 *Pinky's Goose Is Cooked* 94

Chapter 23 *A Flaming Temptation* 99

Chapter 24 *The Valley of Confusion* 103

Chapter 25 *Short, Mean, and Tricky* 109

Chapter 26 *Emma and the Bee* 114

Chapter 27 *These Boxes Bite* 117

Chapter 28 *Peka Makes a Move* 121

Chapter 29 *Ina Hangs* 126

Chapter 30 *Now It Begins* 130

Chapter 31 *One Down* 133

Chapter 32 *Driving with Dinosaurs* 137

Chapter 33 *The Unstoppable Bull* 142

Chapter 34 *Book 'Em, Eddie* 144

Chapter 35 *The Darkest Hour* 148

Chapter 36 *The Worst Possible Thing* 150

Chapter 37 *Where's Eddie?* 158

Chapter 38 *War of the Words Part 1: Ignorance in Charge* 162

Chapter 39 *War of the Words Part 2: The Amazing Eddie* 167

Chapter 40 *Three Heroes* 174

About the Author 177

Acknowledgments

Few books come to be without the efforts of many people. This book, however, has had the benefit of a team of advisors, artists, and educators dedicated to its vision, story, and mission of literacy, from the very beginning. *Aloha Island* would not exist without their involvement.

Sincere thanks to Brooke Loughridge and Erin Furuya, without whom this project would never have been completed. Also thanks to Lynn Wikoff and Andrea Cascardi, who provided expert editing, laser-beam focus, and grace under pressure. And thanks to Boni Gravelle for her guidance and perspective from her years in the classroom.

Most of all, we thank our children: Carson and Chloe Loughridge, Coco and Harry South, and Aidan and Brady Furuya. They were the inspiration for this book, and because they are the true experts on being kids, they were our most trusted advisors.

Map of Aloha Island

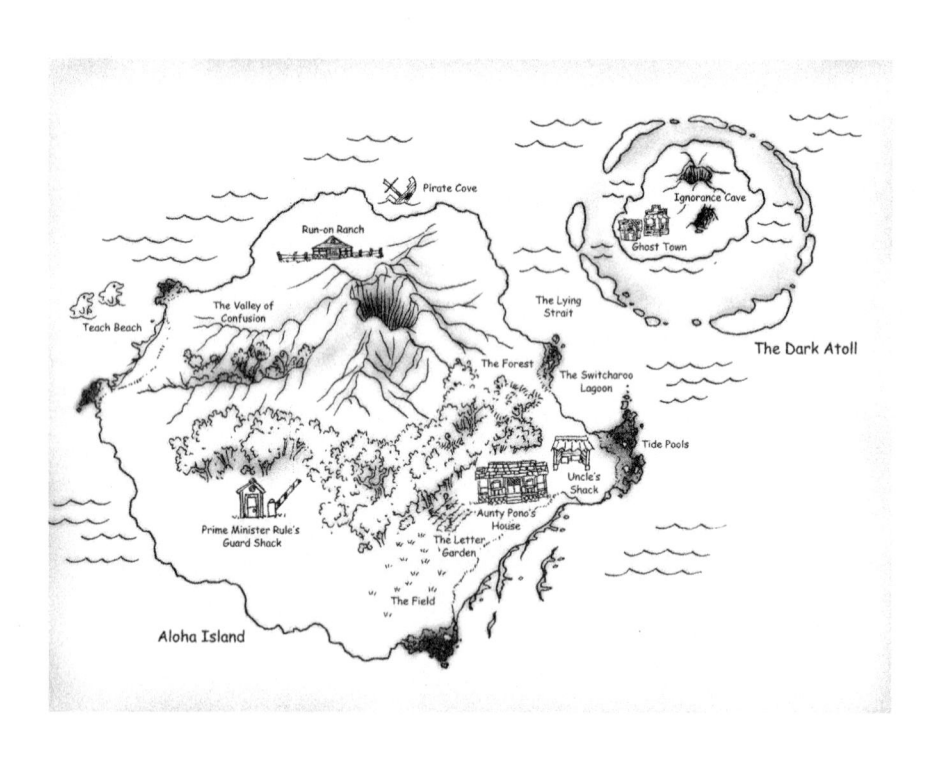

Chapter 1

Ambush

Nine-year-old Eddie Akamai (a-ka-my, which means *smart* in Hawaiian) didn't know what to do. Right now, he was walking to school with his little sister, Emma. At the same time, he wasn't. In his head, huge men chased Eddie across the beach. Their big hands grabbed the air right behind him. Their pounding feet got closer and closer, and Eddie was scared.

One Saturday two years ago, Eddie got to play "spear the fear" on the beach with a big bunch of grown-up fishermen, including the best fisherman of them all—Eddie and Emma's dad, Big E.

"'Spear the fear' is simple," Big E told Eddie. "It's the two of us against all of them. You catch the football and try to run through the other guys and they all try to 'spear' you—like tackle, yeah?"

Eddie nodded.

"I'll block a couple of the guys, but you gotta keep running with the ball as fast as you can, no matter what," Big E said. Eddie nodded again, but all he could think about was how big all the grown-up guys were. The guys had thick, heavy arms. They had tattoos. Big E could see the fear take hold of his son. Eddie would always remember the gentle touch of his father's hands that day as Big E knelt down and took him by the shoulders.

"Fear says you are alone, Eddie. Fear says you are weak," Big E said. "But if you trust yourself and trust those you love, you will never be alone. Then you will be stronger than anything you fear."

But Eddie and Emma's dad, Big E, had died in a car wreck last year. So now Eddie wasn't sure he believed that anymore. Eddie didn't know what to believe. His little sister, Emma, seemed to believe that all you had to do was sing to be happy. She was singing a reggae song she just made up as she skipped along next to him on the way to school. Emma loved reggae, which is a joyful kind of island music, and she loved learning about letters and reading. So she was singing this song with a lot of enthusiasm— which in this case means really loud. Her song went like this:

Hear my alphabet, sister sun
Hear my alphabet, brother moon
A - B - C - D - E - F - G
I sing it for you, I sing it for me
H - I - J - K - L - M - N - O - P
I sing it high up in a tree
Q - R - S - T - U - V - W
I sing it for me, I sing it for you
X - Y - Z
I sing it down below the sea

"Sing it with me, Eddie," Emma said.

Eddie just grumbled and shook his head.

Emma saw Eddie's friend, Kim Kokua (ko-<u>koo</u>-ah, which means *help* or *helper*) waiting for them at the corner like she always did. Kim was the same age as Eddie, but she always made Emma feel like she was Kim's friend, too. So Emma left grumpy Eddie and ran up to Kim, still singing.

Eddie watched Emma run to Kim. He watched Kim sing along and he felt a little better. Maybe Kim could help him figure things out. He walked up to the girls as they finished singing and apologized to Emma for not singing with her.

"No worries, Eddie," Emma said.

Kim looked at Eddie. "What's going on?" she asked.

"I flunked the third grade reading test."

"That's tough."

"They had a meeting with my mom. Today I have to get tested again and start *first grade* reading with a special tutor," Eddie said.

"You'll pick it up soon. I'll help, too, if you want," Kim said. Kim Kokua was not only Eddie's best friend; she was also the smartest kid he knew. She had helped him since first grade by reading his homework to him. And even with her big, thick glasses covered with ocean spray, she was the best surfer he'd ever seen. But the real reason Kim and Eddie were so close was this: from the time they were tiny kids they always told each other the truth.

"I'm not going to school," Eddie said. As soon as the words were out of his mouth, Eddie felt smart and strong. He felt like he was in charge of his own life.

"That's crazy," Kim said.

"I'm not going to let them pull me out of class for baby reading," Eddie said, and after saying that, he felt even stronger.

"You have to keep trying, Eddie," Kim said. "And anyway, if you don't go to school, what the heck will you do all day?"

"He'll go out on little boat *Lulu* and fish!" Emma said, smiling like she had won a guessing game.

"Come on, Eddie, quit fooling around," Kim insisted. "You can't quit school."

"You never quit anything, Eddie," Emma said.

"I'm not fooling around," Eddie said. "I'm being honest. I can't try to read anymore, or talk about trying to read anymore, or even think about trying to read anymore. I've tried since kindergarten and it doesn't do any good. And even if I finally do figure out a word, the next time I look at it, the letters jump around and turn backward and I can't read it again. I'm sick of the whole thing, and I'm sick of everybody in school thinking I'm a moron."

"No one thinks you're a moron," Kim said.

"Yeah, no one thinks that," Emma said.

"Hey, *moron*!"

Emma, Kim, and Eddie all knew who that nasty voice belonged to—Becka Booker. They turned around and looked down the sidewalk.

"Eddie, these bozos don't count," Kim said.

Becka Booker smiled at them from between her two huge cousins who went everywhere she did; Kirby Booker—the toughest kid in the fifth grade, and Big Normy Booker—the biggest kid in the fifth grade, and maybe the whole world. Becka was their leader and the sneakiest, meanest, creepiest, and all-around most completely evil fourth-grader in the entire universe.

Emma wasn't going to let Becka get away with calling her big brother Eddie a moron. She dropped her book bag and ran at Becka with her fists clenched before Eddie or Kim could stop her. Kim and Eddie ran after her, but they were too late. Emma leaped in the air and yelled right in Becka's face.

"My brother is not a moron!" she shouted. "He's smarter than you, you, you...*bozo*!"

Big Normy grabbed Emma by the hair and held her at arm's length. Kirby and Becka laughed. Emma struggled to get free.

"Hey!" Kim yelled, and she started toward them, but Eddie put his arm out and held her back.

"Let my sister go," Eddie said.

"Ooh, help, the moron is scaring me," Becka said with a smirk. Kirby and Big Normy snorted. "My cousins say no, moron," Becka said. "You have to pay us first. All the lunch money any of you got."

Eddie ignored Becka and looked at Big Normy, who was holding Emma. He locked eyes with Big Normy, who didn't like it. "Let her go, Normy," Eddie said, his voice calm, quiet, and very serious.

Big Normy felt Eddie's eyes burning into him and realized Eddie wasn't scared. And since Big Normy was a bully, that scared him. So he let Emma go.

"Run," Eddie said to Emma. "I'll meet you at school." He turned to Kim. "Make sure she gets there safe. Hurry!"

Kim and Emma took off like Eddie said, but they didn't go to school. They went where they figured Eddie would go next.

Kirby grabbed Eddie as Becka yelled at Normy. "This *moron* made you look dumb. What do you do when someone makes you look dumb, Big Normy? What do you *do*?" Big Normy's meaty hand balled up into a fist. "Punch him out!" yelled Becka.

"Punch him out!" yelled Kirby.

Big Normy scrunched up his sweaty face at Eddie and cocked his thick arm back, ready to pound Eddie with his massive fist. But Eddie looked Normy in the eye and didn't flinch. Eddie knew that Big Normy only hit when he knew he would win. Big Normy relaxed his fist and looked at the ground. Becka's whole skinny little body shook with rage. Eddie smiled as he watched Big Normy walk away. But because Eddie was watching Big Normy, he wasn't watching Becka. And that's when Becka stepped up and punched Eddie right in the face.

Chapter 2

Escape

Kumu's (koo-moo's) Grocery stood at the entrance to Kumu's Marina, where Eddie's mom kept the little boat, *Lulu*, that Eddie's dad, and now Eddie, loved to take out fishing. When he wasn't serving customers, Kumu sat tucked away reading in the corner of the store, surrounded by tall shelves that overflowed with piles of books that weren't even for sale. Kumu looked like a mole peeking out of a cave when you went up to pay him for your stuff.

Kumu looked up from the book he was reading when Eddie walked into the store. Eddie went to the refrigerator case in the back for some bottles of water to take out on *Lulu*, but then he saw his face reflected in the glass. His left eye was swollen and turning purple from where Becka had hit him, and suddenly he didn't feel strong or smart or in charge at all.

But he felt smart out on *Lulu*, Eddie thought. Out on *Lulu*, he *could* read—he could read the water. The waves, the wind, the life hidden below the blue, all of it fit together and told him stories of what had happened out there and the different possibilities of what might happen in the near future. The water spoke to Eddie. But letters never told him a thing.

Eddie shook all the thinking out of his head, pulled two big bottles of water from the refrigerator case, and grabbed a box of saltines on the way up to the register.

Kumu pulled himself away from the book he was reading and rang up Eddie's water and crackers. "Want some ice for that eye, Eddie? No charge," Kumu said.

"No thanks," Eddie said. Suddenly he felt tears. *Oh, great,* Eddie thought, *what's that about?* And he turned his head away.

"How's school?" Kumu said.

"It's boring, that's what it is," Eddie said. "All right?"

"All right," Kumu said. "You know, Eddie, I couldn't read a word until I was ten years old. I thought there was something wrong with me. Not true. I'm just wired different. I needed someone to give me a hand. Lucky for me, my aunt was the school librarian."

Eddie turned back to Kumu, his mind racing. *What's going on? How does Kumu know?*

Kumu read Eddie's reaction. "Last time she was in, your mom mentioned you were having a little trouble with reading," Kumu said.

"I'm not having trouble with anything," Eddie said.

"I can help, Eddie. You come by here after school or on weekends and you'll be reading in no time. What do you think?"

Eddie didn't answer. He was thinking, *What's next?* Maybe his mom would start walking up and down the street with a sign that read: "Hey, everybody! My son Eddie is dumber than dirt!"

"Hey, I've got a riddle for you," Kumu said. "What takes you away, makes you pay, gets you a filet, and even more, a place to stay?"†

16

Eddie shrugged. "I don't know," he said, as he edged closer to the door. He really wanted to go. He wanted to get on board *Lulu*, where he could be alone and feel good about himself again. He imagined *Lulu* waiting for him, her red hull bumping gently against the dock, and *Lulu* written in bright yellow letters on the stern.

"A *book*," Kumu said, trying to bring Eddie's attention back to his riddle. "Get it? Storybooks take you away, financial records you call books, you book a table at a restaurant and—"

"Yeah, I get it, I get it," Eddie said. "And thanks, but I don't need help. I'm smart enough."

"Of course you're smart, Eddie. It has nothing to do that," Kumu said.

But Eddie was already out the door and running down the dock to where *Lulu* was waiting. And when he got to the end of the dock, again things weren't as he planned. Kim and Emma were sitting in the boat. They looked up at him and waved.

"Hi, Eddie," Emma said.

"What are you doing here?" Eddie said.

"We saw what happened with that sneaky cheater Becka," Emma said.

"And since we knew you'd come here, we decided to meet you," Kim said.

"Why?" Eddie asked.

"Because Emma's your little sister and I'm your best friend, and we care about you," Kim said.

"Yeah," Emma said, "we care about you. And we hate that lame-o Becka."

"Please come back to school," Kim said.

"No way," Eddie said, as he jumped into the boat. Soon he had started the motor.

"Fine," said Kim, "we'll go with you."

"Yeah, fine with me, too," said Emma.

"Fine," said Eddie.

Eddie hadn't figured out where he was going to go or how long he'd be gone when he first headed for the boat. But now, with Kim and Emma along, he thought he'd better just putter around the harbor for a few minutes to save face and come back in. And then what? Eddie was miserable. There was just no way out of this mess he was in.

So the three kids, as stubborn as three stones, motored out into the harbor under a gray, drizzly sky. Then an extremely strange thing happened. The sky lightened, but only in one spot, right above their boat. The waves grew still and the light grew warm and golden, but only in a tight circle right around them. Then, with a terrifying rush and roar of wind and water, the little boat *Lulu* was floating in what looked and felt like a golden soap bubble. And *Lulu*, carrying three stunned and mystified kids, began moving out of the protected waters of the harbor, and try as he might, there was nothing Eddie could do to stop it.

Outside the harbor, the bubble moved faster and faster, taking them farther and farther out into the open ocean as Eddie, Emma, and Kim held on to *Lulu* and each other for dear life.

Chapter 3

The Bubble Bursts

"Are we going to be OK, Eddie?" Emma squeaked, squeezing Eddie's hand. The golden bubble flew fast a few feet above the water. The waves and clouds outside the bubble sped by in a blur. The skin of the bubble shimmied a little and suddenly began to slow down. The boat slammed against the water once, then again. Eddie could smell the ocean.

"Emma! Kim! Hold on tight!" he yelled, as he grabbed the wheel.

They slammed into the water a third time. The bubble popped with a *bang* and suddenly, waves as tall as buildings were roaring around *Lulu*. But Eddie got the outboard running and turned *Lulu*'s bow into the angry walls of dark water that rushed at them. Each time, just as it seemed they would be swallowed whole by the swirling ocean, *Lulu* would ride up to the top of the foaming water, and they could get a glimpse of the wild sea surrounding them. It went on for miles.

The next instant, they dropped down the back of the wave while the angry wind howled in their ears. Eddie kept his hands on the wheel of the boat and concentrated on steering them into the waves and keeping them safe. Kim held on to the boat with one hand, and held Emma close to her with the other. Emma was too scared to move an inch. She held on to the seat in the boat with both hands as tight as she could.

Emma wanted to help Eddie and Kim. She knew she was smart and strong, and she was sure she could do something, but couldn't think what because being scared stopped everything. Sometimes Emma felt big and brave, like when she defended Eddie and jumped up and yelled in Becka's face. But sometimes she felt small and helpless.

Then Emma remembered a nightmare that had made her wake up screaming. Her mom came in and told Emma that a bad dream was just a story. And since it was a story, she could change it to make it good. "So, now when you have bad dreams," her mother had said, "you don't have to be scared. Because if you can write your own story…"

"You can write your own happy ending," Emma said. So, still scared, and holding on to the seat with both hands, she started to sing, almost in a whisper.

> *Hear my alphabet, sister sun*
> *Hear my alphabet, brother moon*
> *A - B - C - D - E - F - G*
> *H - I - J - K - L - M - N - O - P*
> *I sing it high up in a tree*
> *Q - R - S - T - U - V - W*
> *I sing it for me, I sing it for you*
> *X - Y - Z*
> *I sing it down below the sea*

When the boat raced down the back of the biggest wave yet, and the wind turned the sea spray into stinging needles, Emma smiled because singing her song made her feel strong. And because she felt strong, she looked out at the scary big waves. She saw an even bigger wave coming from behind the boat, and that wave had an *eyeball* in it. And the eyeball *winked* at her.

"Eddie!" Emma screamed. "Eddie! *Look out!*"

Emma broke away from Kim, and ran into her big brother with such force that Eddie lost his grip on the wheel. *Lulu* fell off the back of the wave, slammed sideways into the sea, and nearly capsized, which would have been a very bad thing for sure.

But they didn't capsize. As a matter of fact, Emma probably saved all their lives, because at the exact moment the little boat *Lulu* fell off the wave, the wave crashed into huge, impossibly tall rocks that had been hidden in mist and low clouds.

Emma held on to Eddie and tried her best not to cry. "I'm sorry Eddie, I'm sorry, but…I saw, behind us…"

Eddie hugged Emma with one arm and steered them away from the huge rocks with the other. Then the low clouds lifted and the rocks looked more and more like a wall made out of really big lava rocks. Eddie, Kim, and Emma stared at the wall. It looked as high as the sky and stretched as far as they could see.

"What is it?" Kim asked. "And where are we?"

"I don't know, and I don't know," said Eddie. His first thought was that maybe they had been blown to one of the neighboring islands. But the more he looked at this thing, the more he knew that whatever it was, it wasn't anywhere near Hawaii.

"*Eddie!*" Emma screamed, even louder than before. She pointed out to the sea. "There! There it is! The wave with the *eye!*"

Eddie's and Kim's mouths dropped open. Emma was right. A towering gray wave, with a huge, unblinking eye smack in the middle of it, was heading right for them.

Chapter 4

Biggie Brings It

Before Eddie could steer away, the wave stopped right next to the boat. The eye blinked. And it stared at the three of them. Then a blast of warm air and stinky water shot straight out the top of the wave. It wasn't a wave with an eyeball after all. It was an extremely large humpback whale.

The raging sea became calm and the roaring wind turned into a gentle breeze. But still, now they were stuck in the middle of the ocean between a huge humpback whale and a huge lava rock wall. Then the whale talked to them.

It wasn't "talk" like he sat up and moved his lips or made words come out of his blowhole or anything. He communicated, as humpback whales always do, with his songs.

Eddie, Kim, and Emma sometimes heard haunting whale sounds echoing through the ocean when they went snorkeling. But the amazing thing with this humpback whale was that they could understand what he was saying. The meaning of what he said rumbled through their bodies and they just knew. And even more amazing, somehow he understood *them*. He said his name was Biggie Large, and at forty-five feet long and weighing thirty-five tons, he was the biggest living thing the kids had ever seen.

Biggie had been heading up to Alaska when he heard Emma's song through the water, and he had to find out who was making "that righteous sound." Maybe Eddie could accept that, but then Biggie said the huge lava rock wall that loomed out of the ocean right behind them wasn't there at all. What was there, Biggie said, was the Line of Enchantment that protected the magic world of Aloha Island. The kids saw a lava rock wall because that was the way their minds could accept it. Biggie smiled, and the water around them hummed with a deep beat coming out of his body. Emma and Kim stood up in the boat, moving to the groove. Even Eddie nodded his head to the rhythm. Then Biggie laid his lyrics on top like this:

> *As I float in the ocean thinking all I don't know*
> *I realize there's only one place that I gotta go*
> *I've been resisting the truth I know since forever*
> *So my head won't accept even one single letter*
> *Time to start my reading now when Aloha Island shows me how.*
> *Time to start my reading now when Aloha Island shows me how.*

By now, Emma and Kim were really into it and sang along on the chorus. As they sang, Biggie led them to an archway that opened on crystal blue water.

"There you go, kids. Keep her straight on until you bump into Aloha Island," said Biggie. "But remember, things are a lot different over there. They don't call it a magic island for nothing."

"Things have been plenty different already," said Kim. "Thanks for helping us out."

"Yeah," said Emma, "and that was a great song."

Biggie puffed up with pride and blew air and spray out of his blowhole. "Thank you, my little one," he said. "Oh, and I dropped the second stanza lyrics into your head. Sing them on your way to Aloha Island and you'll get a surprise. Something fun, I promise."

"You dropped them into my head?" said Emma.

"A little humpback magic," said Biggie.

Eddie steered *Lulu* through the arch and into the waters of Aloha Island.

"All right, when we get to Aloha Island, or whatever it is," said Eddie, as he pushed the throttle forward, "we'll just call home, get gas and directions, and go back to Honolulu."

Kim spotted the speck of a brilliant green island far in the distance. "That must be Aloha Island over there."

Chapter 5

The Letter Drop

K im dangled her legs over the rail of *Lulu*'s bow. "Kim!" It was Emma, doing the loudest, closest ear whisper in history.

"Ow," Kim said.

"Sorry," Emma said. "But I don't want Eddie to hear." Kim glanced at Eddie, who was back by the wheel looking out at the water. Emma scooted closer. "Biggie said if I sang the second verse now, we'd get a fun surprise."

"Didn't Eddie tell you not to?" Kim asked.

Emma shrugged. "Yeah, I know. So it'll surprise him. C'mon, Kim. Please sing it with me."

Kim was about to say she didn't know the words, when all of a sudden she did. *That's magic for you*, she thought. Then, drumming on the side of *Lulu*, she joined right in with Emma, singing the second verse of the Biggie song at the top of their lungs.

As I think of the letters and the sounds that they make
It hits my head each is different and that you can't fake
Letter names and their sounds are different as can be
Tell me, does it fool you? It doesn't fool me!
So listen up when the letters tumble down
And the music of their sounds goes around and around

*Now **A** sings out **a**, **B** sings out **b**,*
*C sings out **c**, and **D** does that **d**, **d**, **d**.*
*When **E** sings out **e**, **F** sings out **f**,*
*G sings out **g**, and **H** does that **h**, **h**, **h**.*
*So **I** sings out **i**, **J** sings out **j**,*
*K sings out **k**, and **L** does that **l**, **l**, **l**.*
Tell me can't you see
What the written word can be
The books we write and read
Will be about you and me
Time to start my reading now when Aloha Island shows me how.
Time to start my reading now when Aloha Island shows me how.

As the girls rapped and sang through the alphabet, the sky clouded over, a breeze swept across the boat, and it started to rain. But it didn't rain raindrops. It rained tiny raindrop alphabet letters. They looked like little water balloons. When a letter landed on the boat, it made its own letter sound.

By the time Emma and Kim started in on the chorus of the song, the rain was singing along with them.

When the girls had started singing, Eddie was at *Lulu*'s wheel concentrating on getting them to shore safely. When the raindrop letters began to fall, he was just as amazed at the sight as the girls, and nodded along with the beat of the song. Then, the little boat *Lulu* came to a sudden, dead stop.

Chapter 6

Trouble Right Off the Bat

Lulu ran aground on the white sand beach of the most unusual tropical island the kids had ever seen. Everything on the island glowed with a shimmering warmth. It reminded Emma of how her dreams looked when she was sick with a fever. Which wasn't exactly bad, but Emma thought it might not be exactly good, either. Still, it was an astounding sight. A towering volcano stretched up from the center of the island into the perfect blue sky. And a rainbow sparkled above the volcano like a great big welcome sign.

The rainbow even said, "Welcome," out loud.

At least that's what Emma thought, so she smiled at the rainbow and said a polite, "Thank you."

But a crabby voice answered, "Not up *there*, you silly goose, down *here*. When's the last time you heard a rainbow talk, for Word's sake?"

The three looked over the side of the boat to see not just a crabby voice, but (what else?) a crab staring up at them. He carried a tiny book under his arm. Eddie couldn't stop staring. It was one thing to have a whale talking to you. It was a whole other thing to see an irritated crab moving his mouth and talking while he stared back at you with his tiny eyes waving around on the ends of little wiggly stalks.

"Throw me a line," he said. "I'll pull you the rest of the way onto the beach. And stop gawking at me. It is both rude and impertinent, though I don't know what else I should expect from human children. The name's Charley, not Chuck or Chucky, though both are also variants of the root name Charles. Now throw me that line like I told you."

Emma threw Charley the line and he did pull *Lulu*, with all three of them aboard, the rest of the way to the beach.

"Is this...uh, Aloha Island?" Eddie asked.

"Well, *of course* this is Aloha Island. Are you human beings or nincompoops?" Charley said, rolling his eye stalks all over the place. "Where did you think you were, the moon?"

The three kids shared another glance. At this point, anything was possible. But Charley told them to quit acting like children and shake a leg. They had to get to the house.

Eddie, Kim, and Emma followed Charley Crab off the beach onto a flagstone path. It wound up a grass-covered hill that rose up to a small white wooden house fronted by a wide lanai (lah-<u>nye</u>, which means a covered porch in Hawaiian) that faced the ocean below. A warm breeze rustled through a stand of palm trees shading the sturdy tile roof. Deep red window boxes on the house and bright blue planters on the lanai were overflowing with the most colorful and oddly shaped flowers any of the kids had ever seen.

As they walked along the path, Eddie, Emma, and Kim had the uncomfortable feeling that they were being watched. But they didn't see anybody around besides the crabby Charley Crab skittering sideways ahead of them. And as soon as they reached the house, he disappeared under the steps of the lanai without a word, leaving them all alone.

Chapter 7

Someone's in the Kitchen

The three kids looked around. There wasn't a sound. The feeling that they were being watched got stronger. They edged closer together. Then Eddie looked at Emma and Kim. "What the heck are we afraid of?" he said.

"I don't know," Emma said.

"Nothing," Kim said.

"OK," said Eddie, "let's see if anybody's home."

When they took the first step up to the lanai, the front door swung open with a *bang* and a bright ball of energy exploded at them with a giant *whoosh*. Then the air around them filled with excited laughter. Standing in front of them was a short, round woman wearing a straw garden hat covered with ribbons, a rainbow-colored muumuu (a loose-fitting, comfortable dress), and a thick lei of odd-shaped flowers around her neck.

"Oh, I'm so sorry, I meant to come down and greet you at the shore myself, but I was putting up *p*'s in the kitchen and lost track of the time. And now look, I'm forgetting my manners. I am Aunty Pono, but you just call me Aunty, OK?"

"It's good to meet you," Eddie said. "I'm—"

"Oh, no need for introductions," Aunty Pono said. "Welcome to Aloha Island, Eddie and Emma Akamai, and Kim Kokua."

A small scarlet-colored bird with a long yellow beak landed on Aunty Pono's shoulder and tilted its head at the children. "Welcome," said the bird.

"This is my friend Ina the I'iwi (ee-<u>ee</u>-wee) bird," Aunty Pono said. "Come on in, everybody wants to meet you." She gave them a big, shining smile. "We'll have some Letter Lemonade. You must be all done in after that boat trip."

Emma thought that Aunty's little house was the most beautiful house she had ever seen. Emma saw that the oddly shaped flowers in the planters and window boxes were actually little letters. There were pale green *p*'s, aqua blue *q*'s, warm yellow *w*'s; every letter in the alphabet in every color you could imagine.

As Aunty brought them into her sunny kitchen, Kim caught that same scent of fresh flowers from on board *Lulu*. The scent came from the thick lei around Aunty's neck. Kim noticed that the brightly colored flowers were letters. Strung together in Aunty Pono's lei, they made words, and the words strung together made sentences. To top it off, the letters, words, and sentences kept changing right in front of her eyes.

"Aloha Three Kids!" it read one minute, then the lei flowers changed to, "We sure need you!" And in the blink of an eye, it changed again to, "Pretty freaky, huh?"

Aunty Pono noticed Kim staring at her lei. "Don't pay too much attention to my lei, Kim," Aunty said. "It's a little mischievous sometimes." Just then, the lei spelled, "Look out behind you!" Both Kim and Emma spun around, only to see the lei spelling, "My, you are odd children," when they turned back.

"Behave!" Aunty Pono said, as she gave the lei a little shake. The lei spelled, "Sorry," then a second later, "No, I'm not," and the girls broke into giggles.

Charley Crab jumped up on to the table next to Eddie and patted Eddie's hand with his claw. "I'm glad to see focus on the part of the oldest of your group. Strong focus, that's what we need around here. It doesn't do to get distracted by nonsense like that spelling lei."

"It has nothing to do with focus," Emma whispered. "My brother has a hard time reading."

"That can't be!" cried Charley, skittering backward and knocking over a bowl of freshly shelled sweet *p*'s, which made "*p - p - p*" sounds as they bounced on the red-and-white checked tablecloth.

Ina the I'iwi bird fluttered off Aunty's shoulder. She flew into a jar of *t*-bags by the kettle, spilling them on the floor with a chorus of "*t - t - t*" sounds. Emma, startled, stood up from the table, and the back of her chair tipped over the bag of chocolate-dipped *r*'s on the counter that Aunty was saving for tonight's dessert. They made a whole bunch of round "*r - r - r*" sounds as they rolled into the kitchen sink.

"Oh, for Word's sake!" Aunty Pono said. "Everybody please calm down!" The sharpness of her tone stopped all in their tracks. They turned their attention to Aunty.

"To begin with, Charley Crab, I am shocked that you, of all creatures, would be so rude to one of our guests."

Charley looked properly sheepish, which in this case means embarrassed, and not actually looking like a sheep. This is also true in the reverse if you should call an especially irritable sheep "crabby."

Anyway, back in Aunty Pono's kitchen, Charley stood among the spilled *p*'s, and apologized to Eddie. Kim thought how cute Charley looked holding his little claws together in front and bending his eye stalks down toward the tablecloth.

Before Eddie could reply, a high, piercing squeak filled the air, "Fearless Fur-Ball to the rescue!" And an enthusiastic young brown bat flew into the kitchen and right into a string of *d*'s drying in the window. They rained down on the windowsill with deafening "*d - d - d*" sounds as the bat screeched, "Not my fault!"

Before Aunty could get things settled down, Ina and Charley had knocked into the *p*'s and *t*'s again, and though Emma kept her seat, she did jump a little and more *r*'s rolled around, which got some *b*'s bumbling on a shelf going "*b - b - b*" and cold *c*'s in the refrigerator going "*c - c - c*." By the time the *f*'s in the freezer got going, and the *w*'s and *g*'s in the window garden joined in, along with the normally calm *l*'s in the Letter Lemonade, every consonant in the kitchen was popping off.

While Aunty was busy getting some excitable *x*'s back into their box, the bat flew right up to Eddie and started flapping his wings. "There's no need to fear! Batbat is here," he screeched.

Charley jumped up from the table and tried to grab one of Batbat's wings with a claw to pull him down.

"Get down here!" Charley yelled. "You're being rude and impertinent!"

The bat ignored Charley and kept just out of his reach. Eddie looked at the bat flapping right in front of his nose. The bat smiled a little toothy smile. Eddie noticed the bat had a paperback book clutched in one of his claws.

Eddie pointed to it. "What's that?"

"My comic book about Batbat, a superhero," the bat squeaked. "Want to read it?"

"Uh…no thanks. Maybe later."

Eddie usually avoided any reading situation. When he was asked to read out loud at school, he would feel his face flush and he'd duck his head down without saying a word. But Eddie had felt different from the minute he stepped onto this island. The letters here flipped around on him when he tried to look at them, just like back at school. But it didn't bother him or make him feel like a moron. Maybe that was because the letters here seemed to flip and jump around like it was normal. And they made those cool sounds. Eddie didn't know if he could trust this place or how he felt, so he kept this to himself for now.

Kim noticed that Eddie had that open, curious look in his eyes that he usually had only out on the water. "How come everybody seems to know who we are?" she asked.

Right then, at the other end of the kitchen, a door opened and Aunty Pono's brother, Uncle Aka stepped in. He wore a headset with a microphone that was wired to an open laptop computer he was carrying on his left arm.

"My sister didn't tell you yet, huh?" he said, as he walked up next to Aunty Pono. " We need the three of you to defeat the forces of Ignorance and save Aloha Island from being destroyed." And then he smiled.

Chapter 8

You Want Us to WHAT?

Emma looked at Uncle with her mouth open. "We can't do that stuff," she said. "We're *kids!*"

Kim nodded in agreement. "Emma's right. It sounds like you need people who have some experience in saving islands and things from destruction. Like maybe the Marines."

"Yeah," Emma said, "or knights, or wizards, maybe, since you have all this magic going on around here. It is magic, isn't it? The animals talking and everything? I mean, Biggie Large showed us the Line of Enchantment."

Uncle Aka grinned. "Oh, you met bruddah Biggie? A big talent, that one, and he's real people, isn't he?"

"Well, for a whale, I guess so," Emma said.

"The point is," Kim said, "not one of us is a knight, wizard, or Marine, and really, we were just out for a little boat ride in the harbor when we got plopped over here somehow, and that was hours ago."

As Kim talked to Uncle Aka, Emma joined Batbat and Ina the I'iwi bird by the kitchen door, and they all nodded eagerly to something Charley Crab was saying. Without notice, all four slipped quietly out the kitchen door.

"So, we're sorry," Kim continued to Uncle Aka, "but we really have to get back home before our families get worried and send the Coast Guard out looking for us."

Uncle Aka took a moment to consider what she'd said. "So, Kim," Uncle Aka said, "what you're worried about is time."

"Yes, I am, Uncle Aka," she said. "It's time we got back home. All we need is a little gas for the boat." Why she was the one was having this argument, Kim had no clue. She elbowed Eddie.

Eddie didn't look up. He was absorbed in tapping one of the green *p*'s on the table to make the *p* sound, then tapping a green *t* to make the *t* sound, and repeating the sounds quietly to himself in turn. "*P - t, p - t,*" he said.

"Eddie, we need to go, right?"

But Eddie was now sounding out two new letters on the kitchen table. "*P - o - t,*" he said, "**pot**." Then, "*P - a - t,* **pat**."

"There, Eddie," said Aunty Pono. "You're reading."

Eddie looked up at Kim. "We can go later," he said. "I'm…um…"

"You're reading," Kim said.

"No, I'm just…goofing with letters," Eddie said.

"Eddie, you're giving reading another try. And I think that's great, you know I do," Kim said. "But why *now*, all of a sudden?"

"What are you talking about?" Eddie said. "What's wrong?"

"Nothing," Kim said. "It's just after running away, and all the talk about never going to school for the rest of your life, then taking the boat and risking our lives in a hurricane, now you're all, 'Oh, never mind, I think I'll try reading again after all'? Was this whole terrifying trip a big fat waste of time? I think Emma and I deserve to know. Right, Emma?" she said. "Emma?"

Kim looked over at the table where Emma had been sitting with that bat just a minute ago. But now Emma wasn't there. Emma wasn't at the table, or under the table, or anywhere else in the kitchen that Kim could see.

"Emma!" Kim called out, trying not to sound as worried as she felt. "Emma, where are you?"

Chapter 9

Tempest in a Tide Pool

Charley Crab led the way on the path, while Batbat was telling Emma and Ina all about writing his comic book. "See, I want to be a superhero who's a bat, but there's already a Bat*man*, and besides, I'm a bat, so now I'm Bat*bat* and my comic book, BATBAT: *The Flying Fur-Ball Who Knows No Fear,* is all about my adventures."

"You have real adventures?"

"Not exactly," Batbat said. "I make them up."

"But they're real in your head, yeah?" Emma said. "That's just as good."

Batbat grinned. "Yeah," he said, "that's right."

Charley interrupted, stopping them at the edge of the beach. "Calm down," Charley said, "or nobody meets anybody."

Emma looked past Charley and saw a beautiful butterfly fish and a giant shrimp.

"I saw them first!" the shrimp said. A whole cheerleading squad of brightly colored fish made a pyramid and flapped their fins until they fell over onto a bunch of irritable clams that started snapping at everybody.

"Stop cutting in line!" yelled Charley. "It's against the rules!"

"Gee, there are so many rules around Aunty and Uncle's place, it's hard to keep them straight," said a sneaky-sounding voice behind Charley.

Charley turned. It was Peka (peh-kah, which means *tattler* in Hawaiian) Mongoose, and her sidekick, Kolohe (koh-lo-hee, which means *naughty*) Cockroach. Kolohe was sitting on the back of the third member of their gang, Nunu (noo-noo, which means *greed* in Hawaiian) Pig.

"I'm hungry," Nunu grunted.

Ina squawked in terror and flew back toward Aunty and Uncle's house. Charley, trying not to look nervous, turned to Peka and her gang. His eyes waved around on the ends of their stalks like they always did when he got angry, or scared. "Go away," he said in the gruffest voice he could come up with. "Go back to the dump where you belong. This is a private meeting."

"Don't look like no meetin' to me," said Kolohe Cockroach. "Is this a meetin', Peka?"

Peka Mongoose chewed her toothpick and smiled. "Maybe it is, Kolohe. It sounds to me like Charley's got somebody to introduce to us. That right, Charley?"

Charley skittered right up to Peka's feet. "No! Leave us alone!" he shouted up at her.

Emma started to step out from behind the mango tree, but Batbat stopped her. "Stay down. You don't want them to see you," Batbat said. "These are the bad guys."

But Peka was looking at the I'iwi bird heading to the house. "That bird gets on my nerves," Peka mumbled to herself. Then she turned her attention back to Charley. "We gotta go. But don't worry, Charley, we'll find out what's going on here. And when we do, we'll do something about it. Won't we, fellas?"

Chapter 10

The Dark Atoll

Uncle Aka smiled at Kim and told her not to worry, Emma couldn't have gone far. "C'mon, let's take a look around the house," he said.

As soon as Uncle and Kim stepped outside, Ina came screeching up to them. As near as Kim could figure out, the bird was yammering about illiterate pigs and cockroaches, and some wild mongoose gang. Then, just when Uncle got the bird to calm down, Charley Crab skittered by their feet, mumbling about the gall of some creatures on this island, followed by Batbat and Emma.

Emma stopped long enough to look up at Kim and say, "This is the most exciting and fun place in the whole world!" Then she ran into the house after Batbat.

"What was that all about?" said Kim.

"Not too much," said Uncle Aka. "They bumped into our local troublemakers. That bunch is basically harmless. Why don't I show you around?" Uncle led her to the back of the house. "You're worried about time, aren't you?" he asked.

"We have to get back," said Kim. "People will be worried."

"You and your friends can leave anytime you want to," Uncle said. "But even if you stay on Aloha Island for a month, it won't amount to a second of your time back home."

"That's impossible," Kim said.

Uncle shrugged. "Everything you've seen since your boat got popped into that bubble has been impossible, hasn't it?"

Kim stopped for a second and looked at Uncle Aka. "Yeah, it has."

"It took a little magic," Uncle said, "but your friend Eddie is in there sitting with Aunty Pono and having fun with what's right in front of him instead of worrying that he's too dumb to learn. He wasn't lying to you before."

"I guess you're right," said Kim.

Uncle smiled and nodded as they walked past blossoming vowel trees and consonant cluster bushes, all bursting with wild varieties of colors and shapes. Across a patch of soft green lawn, a lush garden was laid out with row upon row of colorful letter and word plants. More lawn rose up a gentle slope to the edge of a deep green forest. Multicolored birds with extravagant plumes and tails sailed and ducked in and out of the towering trees. In the distance, a few puffy clouds formed a ring around a dignified volcano.

Kim noticed two carved white stones, each about the size of a loaf of bread, set in a semicircle. There was a jagged hole in the lava bed where a center stone would have been, the only scar on a beautiful landscape. Kim wondered what had happened there.

As they walked to Uncle's workshop, Kim stopped in her tracks. She stared out across the cove. A spot of land was visible in the distance. It was a jagged piece of land surrounded by a coral reef, the remains of an island that had mostly sunk beneath the ocean. The place was dark, and she couldn't help but think it ugly. Gray clouds swirled around what was left of the squat volcano at its center. There was nothing green or alive to be seen. The ocean crashed against the island's shoreline like it was trying to wash it away. Kim felt a cold shiver go down her spine and she turned away.

"The Dark Atoll," said Uncle Aka. "That's where the forces of Ignorance have won. If we don't get help, Aloha Island is next."

Kim glanced again at the frightening, desolate atoll, and then turned back to Uncle. "That place used to be like Aloha Island?" Kim asked.

Uncle Aka nodded.

"That's going to happen here?" Kim's gesture swept over all the beauty she had just begun to absorb.

"That depends on you."

And he walked away, leaving Kim looking out over the bay. Maybe, Kim thought, she and her friends could help Aloha Island. Even if they didn't have any special powers, seeing the Dark Atoll convinced Kim that they should at least try. Kim shook the grim image of the atoll from her head and looked around for Uncle.

Uncle Aka tapped on his laptop in an open garage space. It was shaded by a yellow awning, and the building had a bunch of extra rooms and storage areas built onto it every which way. "Uncle Aka's Workshop" was painted in neat blue letters on a lacquered pine board hung on the back wall.

Uncle waved Kim over. Fantastic machines, lab equipment, and overflowing bookcases crowded in with blowtorches, boomerangs, and bunches of junk. It was the coolest place Kim had ever seen. Uncle opened a huge cabinet and Kim saw hundreds of alphabet letters in a stunning range of color patterns and fonts, all floating in hundreds of small bottles of seawater.

"This is my specialty," Uncle said, "Ocean Letters. They come in countless varieties."

"Wow!"

"I can use some help with organizing and sorting them."

"Sure, I'd love to," Kim said. And then she noticed a framed picture of a beautiful young woman among Uncle's things and picked it up. "Who's this?"

Uncle smiled and took the picture from Kim, and gently placed it back on the shelf. "Before we do that, I think you better meet everybody in the Switcheroo Lagoon." He took off his apron and yelled out, "Charley! Charley Crab!"

And just like that, Charley Crab flew out of a sand hole where he'd been napping, like he'd been popped out of a toaster. "Yes, sir! What? Who?"

Uncle laughed as he took off his apron. "It's about game time, isn't it, Charley?"

"Yikes! You're right! Let's go!" Charley said, and ran off the beach and disappeared into the water.

Uncle smiled at Kim. "Have you ever breathed water before?"

Chapter 11

The Flaming Illiterates Sneak Up

Peka was a mongoose with a mission—a "make it happen now" kind of gal. She didn't worry about what was right or wrong, or about learning something so you could make a good decision. That stuff was for sissies. Peka led Kolohe Cockroach and Nunu Pig on a shortcut through the forest.

"Why can't we walk on the path like everyone else?" asked Kolohe.

"Yeah," said Nunu, "I'm getting pokies in my hooves."

"And," whined Kolohe, "how come we can't eat any letters all of a sudden?"

"Yeah," said Nunu again. "I'm hungry and I wanna eat letters. There was a perfectly good *q* root back there. And it had a whole vine full of juicy *u*'s wrapped around it."

"Would both of you, pretty please, just for me, *put a lid on it*. I am the brains in this outfit," she continued, leaning into each of their faces. "I am the one with the plan. So I don't need any of your complaints. *Understand?*"

Kolohe scampered up onto Nunu's back. "OK, OK," said Kolohe. "We were just asking—"

"*Don't,*" snapped Peka. She turned back toward Aunty and Uncle's place and peeked through the tall grass at the edge of the forest. She could see the door to Aunty's house across the garden near the Old Stones Place. Just as Aunty's door was opening, and Peka might get a look at Aunty's "guests," Kolohe tapped her on the shoulder. Peka whirled around, barely keeping herself from screaming at the top of her lungs. "*What?*" she hissed.

"The thing is, you see, if we don't know what you plan to do," Kolohe said, as Nunu nodded his big thick head, "then we don't know what to do."

Peka thought her brain might explode from dealing with these two. But she knew if she didn't keep them calm Kolohe might lose his temper, and then Nunu might start roaring and banging about and give them away. "Just do what I say." Her angry hiss now started to squeak around the edges. "*OK?*" She tried to smile.

That smile was the scariest thing Kolohe or Nunu had ever seen. Peka glanced over at Aunty's house, but with the tall grass, she couldn't see clearly. One kid for sure, that batty bat, and then another kid — or was it two? — behind Aunty.

"But is there eating in your plan?" asked Nunu.

"Yes, there's eating," said Peka. "And you both know this. I laid it all out before."

"But," Kolohe continued, holding his chin in a thoughtful way with his top left leg, "I think if you wrote your plan down for us in a book, we might remember it. We could carry it with us. And put in some diagrams."

"What's a diagram?" asked Nunu.

"It's like a drawing," said Kolohe.

"I like a nice drawing," agreed Nunu, and turned to Peka. "Kolohe's right, you should put drawings in the book."

"You can't *read*, you *lunatics*!" screamed Peka, finally completely losing it.

She jumped up and down in front of Nunu and Kolohe, waving her arms around. The way her mongoose eyes were popping out of her head reminded Kolohe of one of those rubber squeeze toys you get at the carnival.

"*None* of us can read!" Peka screamed even louder. "We *hate* reading, we *hate* writing, and we especially *hate books*! Do you get it now? *We are the Flaming Illiterates!*"

Peka stopped. Aunty Pono was looking their way. The three looked at each other wide-eyed and bolted deep into the forest.

****

Over at the Old Stones Place, Eddie and Emma looked to the forest's edge when they heard what sounded like a cat with its tail caught in a door. It stopped abruptly, and once again all they could hear were the gentle chirps and whistles of the island birds. Aunty Pono didn't seem to notice the noise at all. She had, of course, but she wanted Eddie and Emma to stay focused on what was important — the Stones.

"I'm going to tell you the Story of the Stones. This is the key to Aloha Island and its sad sister, the Dark Atoll. Look." She pointed to the two stones set in the lava rock, and the hole in the center. The small area had the quiet dignity of an altar. Aunty Pono placed flower leis around the two remaining stones and then around the hole between them in the lava rock.

"Was there a middle stone?" asked Emma.

Aunty promised that everything would be answered in the Story of the Stones. And they'd hear the story after Eddie and Emma gathered some wild vowels and consonants in the forest for the Letter Luau tonight.

"The forest where that weird sound came from?" asked Emma.

"The very same," said Aunty Pono. "Stay on the path and you'll be fine. Batbat will go with you so you don't get lost."

Batbat fluttered down, perched on Emma's head, and screeched, "Batbat beats bad boy bullies, buddy!" Emma and Eddie burst out laughing.

Aunty told them to hurry. When Kim, Uncle, and Charley got back from under water, they'd want to hear the story, too.

"What? Kim's where? Under water?" Eddie asked, alarmed.

Aunty apologized for not telling them sooner, but while they were busy in the kitchen with Batbat and the letters, Uncle Aka wanted Kim to meet the reef creatures of Aloha Island. So Uncle and Kim had followed Charley the Crab two steps past the tide pool and straight down to a Watery Grave or two.

Chapter 12

A Watery Grave

Kim looked at Uncle like he was nuts. "Of course I've never breathed water before," she said. "Only fish can breathe water."

Uncle led Kim into the water on the edge of the lagoon, then stopped and turned to her. "That's true everywhere in the world, except in the waters around Aloha Island," he said. "In these waters the rules are different. They're magic rules."

Uncle bent over and dipped his head into the water, and Kim did the same, but of course she held her breath. Under water Uncle winked, breathed the water in, and said, "Go ahead, try." And Kim took the tiniest sip of a breath, and then a little bigger one, and then she was laughing, and breathing water just the same as she breathed air.

"Follow me," Uncle said, and kicked away from the edge of the lagoon, with Kim, still laughing and amazed, following right behind. She swam down to the bottom of the lagoon with Uncle Aka, and found herself in a natural stage area filled with every kind and color of reef and lagoon creature in the sea, all cheering and clapping.

"We're just in time for the Switcheroo Championships," Uncle said.

Uncle and Charley Crab pointed out the players. First, Watery Grave the Sea Urchin and Watery Grave Junior, who ran the game, kept score, and tossed up the letters that changed the words.

Pua the Raccoon Butterfly Fish fluttered her tail and little fins. Ollie the Octopus played on his drum. The Butterfly Fish Cheerleaders followed along in tight formation as Hazel the Harlequin Shrimp sang:

> *Letters come and letters go*
> *They make new words*
> *And make a show.*

A village of red and yellow sea anemones bubbled behind Hazel and joined in the chorus:

> *This is the way*
> *You mean what you say.*
> *And you get better the more you play.*

Then the grave voice of Watery Senior rang through the stadium, "Let's…get…ready…to *Switcheroo!*"

Ollie banged the drums. The cheerleaders and sea anemones hummed and swayed. The tension built. Pua, an eager but inexperienced young fish, went first. The urchins threw up three letters that floated in the water in the middle of the stadium: *M – A – T*.

"*M – a – t*," said Pua, sounding it out. And then she put the sounds together, "**Mat**."

Then the urchins knocked out the *T* with a *P*.

"*M – a – p*," sounded out Pua, "**map**."

Then the *A* was knocked out by an *O*.

"*M - o - p*," said Pua, "**mop**."

In a flash it was a *T* instead of a *P*.

Before she could blink, the *P* was an *N*. Wait, was this a trick? The *n* changed the sound of the *o* to a *u* sound. She was pretty sure, anyway. But she had to choose or lose. Switcheroo was no game for babies. She had to go for it.

"*T - o - n*," said Pua, "ton."

Then the *T* was an *S*.

"*S*," she started to sound it out. But she froze. It didn't seem right to her. That wasn't how you spelled the sun in the sky, and suddenly she couldn't believe that the little boy one was pronounced the same as the sky one. How could anyone know the difference?

"Time's up!" said Watery Grave.

"Time's up!" said Watery Grave Junior.

Uncle Aka, Kim, and Charley Crab could tell Pua's confidence was shaken. Then, the game got even harder and faster, with four- and five-letter words, blends, and some that used the silent *e*. Everyone in Switcheroo Lagoon knew it was over when the Watery Graves dropped the *s* from **seat** and threw up a *b* and an *l*, making **bleat**—which is exactly the sound Pua made when Hazel the Harlequin Shrimp was declared the winner of the championship once again.

****

While Kim was down at the bottom of the lagoon being introduced to Hazel and Pua as Uncle Aka's honored guest, up on land, in the middle of the deep, dark forest, Eddie, Emma, and Batbat were lost. And it was starting to look to Eddie like that might be the least of their troubles.

Chapter 13

The Too Far Safari

Eddie's, Emma's, and Batbat's hike into the forest to pick letters for Aunty Pono's Letter Luau started out fine. Sunlight streaked through the leaves and branches of the tall trees, and letters of all shapes and sizes grew everywhere. Eddie noticed something unusual happening with the alphabet letters. It looked like every once in a while each of the letters glowed and then quickly blinked off. *That has to be the sunlight shining off the leaves,* Eddie thought.

Eddie carried a patchwork sack that Aunty said was only for consonants, and Emma pulled an old red wagon with a big birdcage on it. This was for the vowels. Batbat flew the perimeter. He swooped around trees and called out, "All clear!" and, "Bad boy bullies beware!" and, "Batbat here!" every minute or so.

But now, without even realizing how it happened, they were deep in the forest. Batbat swooped down. "No need to fear. I haven't seen a single pirate."

Emma gasped. "What pirates?"

"The ones with the rusty cutlasses ready to cut off our heads!" Batbat said.

Eddie saw Emma looking around at the thick forest surrounding them. "Emma, don't worry. There aren't any pirates."

"How do you know?" she said.

"Aunty Pono would have told us," Eddie said, "wouldn't she?"

"Aunty Pono doesn't know everything," Batbat said. "I was told the pirates come at night, when you're asleep—"

"Please stop," Eddie said. "You're scaring Emma." Eddie tried to change the subject. "So, how do we collect these wild letters we're supposed to bring back?"

"You have to point at the letter and say the sound," Batbat said.

Emma pointed at a glowing *A* and yelled out, "A!" The letter dropped down to her hand and she put it into the vowel cart, where it hopped around in the big birdcage making the *a* sound happily to itself.

Eddie tried his luck with a glowing *B*. He pointed and yelled, "B!" It bounced down into the palm of his hand with a "*b - b - b*" sound and he dropped it into the consonant sack.

Emma and Eddie were having so much fun, they didn't notice they were way deeper in the forest than they were supposed to be. That is, until Eddie tripped over a branch and almost spilled his bag of consonants.

"Wait!" he said, as he looked around. "Where are we? I don't see the path anymore. Batbat?"

But Batbat wasn't there.

"Where is Batbat?" asked Emma, searching the air around them.

"Batbat didn't beware," said a sneaky-sounding voice.

And then, with a mean laugh, Peka Mongoose swung in on a vine and jumped down in front of Eddie and Emma. At the same time, Kolohe Cockroach and Nunu Pig crashed into the clearing behind them, cutting off their escape. Clutched in Peka's paw was a terrified Batbat, tied up with twine and gagged with a tiny bit of cloth stuffed in his mouth.

"My name is Peka Mongoose," Peka said, as she smiled at the stunned Eddie and Emma. "You are prisoners of the most feared and bloodthirsty gang in this forest — the Flaming Illiterates!"

Chapter 14

Fear Is Here

Peka Mongoose, Kolohe Cockroach, and Nunu Pig grinned and giggled, circling Eddie and Emma. Nunu licked his chops over all the letters in the loaded vowel cart and the bulging consonant bag. Kolohe, standing up proudly on Nunu's head, felt that they were finally acting like real outlaws, doing real outlaw stuff.

Emma stepped closer to Eddie and he put a protective arm around her. Emma was surprised that being surrounded by giggling, sneering animals didn't scare her more than it did. Maybe she was getting braver. Of course, it helped that she was standing next to her big brother. And seeing poor little Batbat tied up like that was making her mad.

When he felt that shudder go through his little sister, and looked at the terrified little bat, Eddie remembered the fight yesterday. He had let Becka's "moron" taunts get to him, and then she sucker-punched him. Not this time.

"Keep your mouth shut and your eyes on the leader," his dad had told him once. "Bullies, especially bullies fronting a gang, are cowards. And a coward can't stand it when someone looks at them with a calm eye and sees what they really are." So Eddie stayed quiet and kept his calm eye on only Peka Mongoose.

Peka didn't like Eddie's eyes drilling into her eyes one bit, and she didn't like the determined look on his face, either. It made her legs twitch, as if they were telling her, "Run away! Get out while you can!"

"Maybe you didn't hear me, you sniveling weaklings," said Peka, looking extra fierce as she stared back at Eddie. "We are the Flaming Illiterates, and we are *bloodthirsty!*"

With that, Batbat fainted dead away in Peka's paws.

"You tell us who and how many you are, and what you're doing with Aunty and Uncle, or the bat gets it," Peka said.

"The bat gets what, Peka?" grunted Nunu Pig. "The letters? You said we get to eat them."

"Never mind!" Kolohe Cockroach barked at Nunu. Kolohe figured now it was up to him to save the situation. He jumped over to a nearby tree. Waving a tiny cockroach-sized machete, Kolohe chopped and chopped at a *b* that wasn't ripe. He hacked away and it dropped with an earsplitting squeal all the way to the ground. "*See?*" yelled Kolohe at Eddie and Emma. "We don't wait for these things to glow. We don't sing songs and point. We take what we want. We don't care, we don't share, and we don't scare!" He jumped to a branch hanging right over Eddie and Emma, and waved his machete. "After the bat gets it, we'll keep doing bad, scary outlaw things until somebody starts talking."

"Yeah," said Peka, getting her nerve back. "You think you look like a tough guy with that little black eye of yours. Well, you don't, OK?" But Eddie's stare was getting under her skin.

"Are there three of you?" demanded Kolohe.

Neither Eddie nor Emma said a word, and Eddie kept his eyes on Peka. This gang of bullies was falling apart. It was almost time to make his move.

"OK, you asked for it!" said Kolohe. "The bat's first!"

Waving his tiny machete again, Kolohe flew off the branch toward Batbat, who was still out cold in Peka's paws. Peka held Batbat up toward the cockroach and turned her head, in case whatever happened was gross. But this gang never had a chance.

Eddie knocked Kolohe out of the air with the back of one hand and plucked Batbat out of Peka's paws with the other.

"Get lost," Eddie said. He handed Batbat to Emma, picked up the consonant bag, and grabbed the handle to the vowel cart. "C'mon, Emma. We're going home." Eddie turned around and headed down the path.

Emma followed Eddie, impressed by how he had just handled the Flaming Illiterates. But in the back of her mind she was still worried about pirates. She looked at the thick forest surrounding them. The pirates could be anywhere, she thought, and she and Eddie wouldn't see them until the rusty cutlasses sliced down on their necks.

Chapter 15

The Story of the Stones Part 1: The Spirits' Gifts

Kim, Uncle Aka, and Charley Crab swam to the surface of the lagoon and stepped onto the shore by Uncle Aka's workshop. As Uncle and Charley walked ahead, Kim shook her head in amazement and looked around this sun-soaked tropical island where animals talked and plants sprouted letters and words. Charley the Crab tugged at her ankle.

"Come *on*," he said. "It's time for Aunty Pono to tell the Story of the Stones. You'll never understand anything around here if you miss that."

She followed Charley toward Eddie, Emma, and Batbat, and as she sat down with the group, Uncle Aka went to find Aunty Pono. As soon as he left, Charley lay down for a crabby nap, and the three kids immediately turned to each other. Eddie told Kim that Aunty had said while they were on Aloha Island they were in "magic time," so no matter how much time passed here, it'd be like they weren't gone even a second back in Honolulu. Kim said she had heard the same thing from Uncle Aka and it made her feel better about being away from home.

"Eddie saved us!" Emma told Kim.

"We were ambushed by the Flaming Illiterates!" yelled Batbat, flapping around their heads.

"Ambushed? Are you all right?" asked Kim, now very worried.

"It wasn't a big deal," said Eddie. "They were trying to scare us. And they bat-napped Batbat."

"But I wasn't scared *one bit*," crowed Batbat.

Eddie hid a smile and Emma jumped in, excited. "There were three of them: a girl mongoose, a pig, and a cockroach. And the cockroach pulled a *knife*."

Kim blinked. "A knife?"

"A teeny-tiny cockroach-sized knife," explained Eddie.

"It looked plenty big to me," Batbat said.

Eddie focused on Kim now. "And you went to a lagoon where Aunty said—"

"I could breathe water. It's true," Kim began.

Before Kim could finish, Aunty Pono and Uncle Aka stepped up. The three kids turned toward Aunty in time to see her lei spell out, "Keep still!" and then, "You losers!"

Kim was whispering to Eddie what it had said when Aunty interrupted. "If my lei can't be polite, it might need a time-out in the refrigerator."

"I'll stop," flashed the lei.

"*St - o - p*," sounded out Eddie. "That's a blend. The lei says stop."

Then abruptly the air grew still as Uncle Aka began to chant. Uncle Aka's voice was deep and strong, and sounded like it echoed out of ancient depths of the island. When he finished, Uncle Aka smiled and nodded to Aunty Pono, who turned to the kids and began her story.

"First, you should understand that three is a very powerful number," Aunty said. "Like a triangle, it forms a base of power. There are three stones in this story. Just like there are three primary colors, three wise men, three cheers, and…the three of you.

"So, many years ago when everything was beginning, Aloha Island and her sister island, Mele Island, were very jumpy places. This was long before Mele (<u>may</u>-lay, which means *song* in Hawaiian) became the Dark Atoll.

"Back then, volcanoes were making the land, storms were making waves, and earthquakes were shaking everything up. The few creatures who were around spent most of their time running or swimming from place to place, trying not to be smashed by falling rocks, swallowed by the sea, or pitched into bottomless cracks in the earth.

"Now, two young girl spirits and one young boy spirit took care of Aloha Island and Mele Island at that time."

"Wait," Eddie said, "are you saying these spirits—"

"Yes, Eddie," Aunty said. "They were very much like the three of you. Two of the spirits were even brother and sister. And I am not making this up." Then, after a pause, she said, "Should I continue?"

Aunty smiled as the three children eagerly nodded. She was feeling more confident that they would be the ones to save Aloha

Island. But she had to be careful how she let the three know of the huge task that was facing them.

"The three young spirits felt sorry for the frightened and confused creatures dashing around the islands," Aunty continued, "and so they decided to help them out by giving them a few tips. First, they went to a mongoose. 'We have some very helpful advice that we'd like to present as gifts to the creatures on the islands,' they told the mongoose. 'These gifts will keep them from being afraid and will help them live happy lives.'

"'Oh, no,' said the mongoose. 'The creatures would never accept anything from you young spirits. They would only accept the gifts from somebody they respect. Better you wrap your knowledge in these banana leaves, and I will present the gifts to the creatures as laws.' The spirits said no.

"Next, the three spirits went to a pig, and he said, 'Oh, the rest of the creatures would be frightened by spirits as powerful and wise as you. You should put your knowledge in these ripe mangoes. I will feed them to the other creatures when you are gone.'

"The spirits could see through this, too, and knew that the pig would eat all the knowledge and never share it with anybody. So they told the pig thanks, but no thanks.

"As they walked away from the beach, a cockroach crawled up to them and said all they had to do was wrap the knowledge in something dead and stinky. Then he would hide it safely in a dark cave where no one would bother it.

"Of course, the spirits knew immediately that all the cockroach wanted to do was hide the knowledge until it rotted away. So, as they did with the mongoose and the pig, they told him no. This time, the boy spirit was so mad that he threw a rock at the cockroach, which his sister told him was a very un-spirit-like thing to do.

"'I can't help it,' the boy spirit said. 'The creatures are all so *selfish*.'

"'You know what?' the two girl spirits said. 'You're right.'

"Completely discouraged, and feeling sorry for each other, the three spirits sat on the beach and stared out at the ocean. Then, without warning, everything was quiet. The ocean, the wind, and the volcano weren't making a sound, and the young spirits knew this was not a good sign. They looked up, and their mother the ocean, their father the wind, and their aunty the volcano were all looking at the young spirits, and they didn't look happy.

"'What? Are you going to sit and cry like babies because the creatures didn't jump around all grateful for your presents? Do you want a parade or something?' Mother Ocean and Father Wind roared.

"The spirits shook their heads no.

"'OK then, *here*,' rumbled Aunty Volcano.

"And the volcano spit three balls of hot lava out of her crater, Father Wind shaped them into three stones, and Mother Ocean cooled them and gave one to each of the young spirits. Then the three young spirits were told by Mother Ocean, Father Wind, and Aunty Volcano to each put a gift of knowledge into one of the rocks and then make a symbol on the rock to show what it held.

"So that's what the young spirits did—and then each of the rocks held a special message. The wind took them from their hands, the volcano threw down a lava bed right here, and the ocean placed the three magical rocks in the lava bed. The rocks stayed there giving inspiration and guidance for generations, undisturbed—until the Dark Atoll." Aunty Pono pointed out the two stones with their drawings which looked something like this:

Aunty told them that the one on the left was an ear and meant *listen*, and the one on the right was an open hand and meant *give*. Then Aunty said, "The missing stone in the middle also had a drawing on it." And she drew lines in the sand that looked something like this:

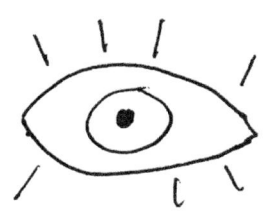

"It was an eye, and it meant *explore*. So together, the Listen, Give, and Explore Stones gave us these things, which were natural to a place that grew letters and words everywhere. The stones told us about listening to stories, reading books to explore, and giving our knowledge to one another by sharing, writing, and teaching."

"What happened to the stone in the middle?" asked Eddie.

"Oh," said Aunty, "that happened not so long ago, and it's the scariest part of the story. It's also why the three of you are here."

Chapter 16

Luau Lunacy

Eddie, Kim, and Emma could hardly wait to hear the rest of the Story of the Stones, especially how they fit in. But Aunty Pono and Uncle Aka stood up and Uncle said, "You'll hear all that soon enough. Right now it's time to get ready for tonight's luau. After everybody's had plenty of eats and plenty of fun, we'll sit down and finish the story." So everybody jumped up and started getting ready for the luau on the big field at the edge of the forest.

****

Inside the forest, the Flaming Illiterates were headed back to the edge of that same big field. Peka Mongoose was afraid that after their failed bat-napping, her gang would never be the same. But being a natural leader, she decided to face the problem and fix it. First, Peka made sure that Kolohe Cockroach hadn't broken any of his legs when he banged into the tree. That took a while because Kolohe had six legs, they stuck out every which way, and neither Peka nor Nunu Pig was sure how to tell if a cockroach's legs were broken in the first place. Plus, with all his hollering and moaning every time Peka touched him anywhere, Kolohe didn't make things any easier.

It turned out that there was nothing wrong with Kolohe at all, but he was sure he had broken *something*, so Peka wrapped the red rag that had been Batbat's gag around Kolohe's head.

They spent what seemed to Peka like forever digging through the grass looking for Kolohe's tiny machete. Then they had to stand around and blame each other for Eddie, Emma, and Batbat getting away. Finally, Peka got the other two Flaming Illiterates to agree to go to Aunty and Uncle's place to "get some answers." Peka, of course, took the lead, and told Kolohe and Nunu she didn't want to hear a meep, a beep, a cheep, or even the teensiest, tiniest whispery little peep from either of them. Peka Mongoose had some serious thinking to do.

If there *were* three visitors, how would she know if they were the three from those old stone stories? And if they were those three, what kind of magic did they have? And then, what was the best way to trap them on the Dark Atoll?

That was a whole lot to think about. So instead, Peka decided to think up something dramatic to call today's adventures. You see, ever since she was little, Peka had liked giving things that happened in her life important-sounding names. The first time she stubbed her toe she called "The Great Peka Foot Ow-ee," and the first time she got lost and found her way back, she named "Peka's Great Re-escape Escape." As Peka marched toward the edge of the forest, she was trying to decide on the important new name for what had happened to her today. Should it be "Peka's Bodacious Bat Battle?" Or "Peka's 'All That' Battle of the Bat?"

Kolohe Cockroach, who had been lying across Nunu's back, moaning, sat up. "Excuse me!" he called out to Peka. "I thought you said no talking!"

Peka was enjoying saying, "Peka's 'All That' Battle of the Bat" over and over. So she didn't hear Kolohe, and when she pushed through a stand of short *A* palms, the branches snapped back and swept the cockroach right off Nunu's back.

"Hey!" screamed Kolohe, as he crashed to the ground and banged his head again.

Nunu was busy looking for something to eat, so he didn't notice, and he followed Peka around the short *A* palms and out of sight.

Kolohe screamed louder, *"Hey!"*

Peka's head popped back through the palms and hissed, *"Shhhhh!"* And then she disappeared.

"One day," Kolohe mumbled, as he brushed himself off, "I'm going to teach that mongoose a lesson."

But Peka didn't hear this, either. She and Nunu were peeking out from behind a big, blue, blossoming *B* bush, and watching Aunty and Uncle's luau from the edge of the forest. There were three kids after all, just like in the prophecy. And they were doing the most amazing things.

****

Eddie, Emma, and Kim were having loads of fun helping set up the luau. Kim and Uncle Aka brought his computer and a bunch of hoses, wires, lights, and machines out to the field. As Kim plugged in cords and screwed machine parts together following Uncle's directions, she asked Uncle what they were making.

He smiled. "This machine is my Wild Word Wrangler. It's an important part of the Letter Luau," he said.

Aunty Pono had Eddie and Emma helping her prepare the luau dinner. Now, being from Hawaii, Eddie and Emma had been to luaus before, and had even helped with the food. But they had never seen food made this way. First, they built a fire under Aunty's big stew pot on the edge of the field near the beach. Then everybody sang a song, which the three kids picked up so quickly it was like they had known it forever. It went like this:

Uncle Aka's tapping his machine
Letters shine like you've never seen
Aunty Pono's stirring her cook pot
She wants to hear you say the word you caught

The fire burned and the water boiled, and Eddie and Emma, along with Batbat, Charley Crab, Ina the I'iwi Bird, and even Pua the Raccoon Butterfly Fish and her friends in the tide pool, sang the chorus of the song as Aunty stepped up to the pot.

Ask all the creatures
Even little fish and baby birds
On Aloha Island
You get to eat your words

Aunty stretched her arms way up, took a deep breath, dropped her head back, and slowly let the air out. As she brought her head forward, she grinned at the creatures and the kids gathered around the pot.

"Ready for Wonderful Wild Word Stew?" Aunty asked. There were excited nods all around. "Remember," she said, "as soon as I've spelled out the food, you have only two minutes to finish gathering the letters, bring them back to me, and say the word. If you succeed, it goes into the pot. If you don't, it doesn't, and we can't have that food until the next luau." Aunty looked over to Kim and Uncle at his card table filled with his computer and strange-looking machines. "All set?" she asked.

Kim picked up the big bag of mumbling consonants and got ready to dump them into a big metal funnel attached to the computer, which was in turn attached to a bright blue hose that led to what looked like an incredibly massive rainbow-colored lawn sprinkler.

Uncle nodded. "All set," he said.

"OK, first letter...*N*!" yelled Aunty Pono.

Kim emptied the big bag of wild consonants into the funnel and Uncle Aka tapped like crazy on his computer keyboard. He threw a switch near the hose. Then the whole contraption made a low rumbling, tumbling, growling noise. The sound grew louder and louder, and Kim stepped back from Uncle's machine, afraid it might blow up.

As she did, she had to jump out of the way of an enormous bubble moving out from the machine through the bright blue hose. When the enormous bubble got to the massive rainbow-colored sprinkler, all the noise stopped. There wasn't a sound, except for the ocean gently washing up on the sand. No one dared move a muscle.

Chapter 17

Few Chew Noodle Stew

Eddie, Kim, and Emma were all pretty sure Uncle Aka's Wild Word Wrangler was going to blow into smithereens, and they were getting pretty scared. But the others around them looked as cool as a crate of cucumbers and kept their eyes on the sprinkler. So they decided to do the same.

Then, with an unbelievably giant *WHOOSH* (which immediately reminded Eddie, Kim, and Emma of the sound the giant bubble had made when it grabbed them and their little boat *Lulu* out of the bay back home), the sprinkler came alive and sprayed the air full of all kinds of brightly colored consonants. Green *T*'s, yellow *B*'s, deep blue *C*'s, and every other color of consonant you can think of floated in easy reaching distance above the ground and the nearby tide pool. Suddenly, everybody was rushing around looking for *N*'s to bring to Aunty.

"Purple *N* dead ahead!" yelled Batbat, swooping out of the sky. He hollered at the *N*, grabbed it as it fell, and dropped it into Emma's hands as she ran toward Aunty. Eddie was right behind her with a glowing red *N* he found floating in the air by the beach.

As kids and creatures rushed toward her carrying all kinds of different-colored *N*'s, Aunty Pono yelled out, "Double *O*'s!" Kim immediately shook all the vowels in the vowel cage into Uncle Aka's funnel, and the sprinkler sprayed sparkling multicolored vowels into the air, where they mixed with the consonants until the night was filled with glowing letters in every color you could imagine.

"*D! L! E!*" Aunty yelled, and creatures and kids dashed everywhere saying the letter sounds at a letter and grabbing it as it fell from the air.

Uncle saw that Kim was eager to join in the fun. "Thanks for your help, Kim. I can handle the rest," he said. "So *go, girl!*"

Kim dashed out just in time to find two orange *O*'s floating by the edge of the forest near where Eddie was saying, "*D!*" to a pink *D*.

Eddie watched as Kim ran up to the orange double *O*'s and said, "**Ooh**," (like the double *o* sound in *toot*). They fell into her outstretched hands. She grinned at Eddie, and the two of them ran their letters back to Aunty Pono at the stew pot. Aunty took the *D* from Eddie and the double *O*'s from Kim, and in the air right above the stew pot, she spelled out the food. It looked like this: **n oo d le**.

Eddie noticed that all the creatures and Kim and Emma were looking at him and smiling, waiting for him to be the first to try and figure it out. "*N*…," he said, starting to sound it out. He was stumped by the double *O*'s. Making the short *o* sound twice in a row didn't seem right, but then he remembered being right near Kim when she said the sound that made them fall into her hand. She had said, "**Ooh**."

For a second, Eddie worried that learning the double *O* sound without sitting down and learning it in a lesson in school might be wrong. But then he remembered again what his dad, Big E, had told him about keeping your eyes and ears open to learning wherever you were.

So he went to the *D* and sounded it out, but got stuck again on the "**le**." But as he sounded out "**nood**" again, Eddie recognized the word as being the same as the word on a box of noodles in Kumu's store, and that he was making the "**nood**" sound in the first part of the word *noodle*. Time was running out, so he decided what the heck and yelled out, "Noodle!"

Everybody cheered, and with a flash the letters turned into a huge bunch of noodles and Aunty dropped them into the stew pot.

Then Aunty yelled, "*P*!" and, "*O*!" and, "*T*!" and, "*A*!" and, "*T*!" and, "*O*!" Everybody laughed and ran across the field or swam around the tide pool yelling out letter sounds, catching shining colored letters as they fell from the air, and running them back to Aunty's stew pot.

****

Peka Mongoose and Nunu Pig were staring through the bushes on the edge of the forest at all the excitement, when Kolohe Cockroach limped up to them.

"You knocked me off Nunu with that branch back there, you know," Kolohe snapped. "I think you sprained my neck."

"Shhh!" shushed Peka, and she turned back to watching the field.

"What's going on?" Kolohe asked Nunu, ignoring another shushing from Peka.

"I don't know," whispered Nunu. "But there are three kids. And it looks like they're having fun."

"No, it doesn't," hissed Peka. "It looks boring. Everything readers do is boring."

"But there are three kids?" asked Kolohe.

"It doesn't matter," Peka grumbled.

"But I thought you said—"

"Remember that lid I keep asking you to put on it? *Put it on!*" barked Peka.

Well, something mattered to Peka, and it was making her nuts. Kolohe decided to ignore Peka as much as possible from now on, and limped over to Nunu.

Nunu reached down with his tusk to help Kolohe up onto his head so Kolohe could be close to Nunu's ear and they could talk without getting yelled at by the nutso mongoose.

"It looks to me like they're having fun," whispered Kolohe. "They're laughing and dancing around."

"And they're making noodle stew. That boy said *noodle* and just like that, there were noodles. Can you do that?"

"No," said Kolohe.

"Neither can I," Nunu sighed. "I wish I could."

"Me, too," said Kolohe. "A nice hot bowl of noodle stew sure would be good right now."

"I like to chew the noodles and the potatoes together real slow," said Nunu.

"I like sucking the noodles in through my lips," said Kolohe.

"Cockroaches don't even have lips," Peka hissed.

Kolohe and Nunu jumped. Peka was standing right next to them, her paws on her little mongoose hips. "I could hear you whispering over here," she said. "You two want noodle stew? I'll get you noodle stew—and a whole lot more. You just wait until these losers fall asleep, and then we'll see who's dancing and singing."

Chapter 18

The Story of the Stones Part 2: Ignorance Attacks

After Eddie, Emma, and Kim finished helping clean up from the luau, everyone gathered back at the Old Stones Place to hear the rest of the Story of the Stones. Aunty Pono brushed a couple of mango leaves away from the hole in the lava bed between the Listen and Give Stones, where the Explore Stone used to be.

"For generations on Aloha Island and Mele Island, the land and sea creatures learned from the stones," Aunty said. "When the tide was low, like it is now, the land creatures would sit with the stones and touch them, or even pick them up and hold them. When they did, they found their heads full of new ideas and insights about themselves and the world around them. When the tide rose, as it will tonight, the stones would be under water. Then the sea creatures could hold the stones and learn from them.

"All the creatures learned how to care for the letters and words that grew on and around the islands. They used the letters and words to share information and stories with one another. Soon they had a library for all the books they were making. There were cookbooks and diaries, dictionaries and storybooks, music books and comic books, picture books and even an encyclopedia. With all the learning and sharing between the creatures, Aloha and Mele

Islands were peaceful and magical places filled with curiosity and energy.

"Then one day, a boat came into the deep bay on the far side of Mele Island. When the people on that boat saw what beautiful islands they had found, they decided to stay. They built a town on Mele Island, and at first the people and the creatures on the islands seemed to get along.

"But as it happens, many of the people who had settled on Mele Island couldn't read. They became suspicious and jealous of the land and sea creatures who could read and write. The settlers began to cut down all the native letter and word trees. The creatures asked the settlers to stop the cutting, but the settlers refused. Instead of the special music of the wind blowing through the narrow stream-filled valleys that gave Mele Island its name, anger and argument filled the air.

"Not all the people were angry. Some tried to get the other settlers to listen to the stories from the library and to the wind's music that sometimes still whispered through the valleys. But in the end, these people were ignored. Suspicion turned to jealousy and the settlers banned reading and writing. And a few of the creatures even joined with the suspicious and angry settlers.

"One night the settlers ran through Mele Island carrying torches and burning every book they could find. 'Reading is boring!' they shouted. 'Ignorance is fun!' they yelled. And they proudly called themselves the Ignorance Army. It was a frightening night for the rest of the people and creatures, who finally decided to get in a sailing canoe and try to escape to Aloha Island.

"But on Mele Island, all the hateful feelings from the Ignorance Army joined with the smoke from the angry torches and burning books and became dark vapors that thickened and grew darker as they rose into the air. The vapors rolled into a nasty cloud that grew darker and thicker and taller, and finally blanketed the entire sky over Mele Island.

"Then there was a flash of lightning and a crash of thunder. Two terrible yellow eyes burned out of the top of the cloud. The eyes searched below like spotlights and found the frightened creatures and people fleeing in the sailing canoe. A rumbling, crashing roar exploded out of the cloud's mouth that was as big as a cave. The cloud had become Ignorance itself," Aunty said, leaning closer to the three kids, "and it was *alive*."

"Oh no!" cried Emma, grabbing Eddie.

Eddie put his arm around his little sister. "It's only a story, Emma," he said. "Don't be scared."

"Yeah," said Kim, taking Emma's hand. "I'm sure it will turn out OK in the end."

"That's right," said Batbat, as he stood on Emma's knee and smiled proudly at all three of the kids. "Now that you guys are here, Ignorance and his pals don't have a prayer."

"You mean he's *real*?" yelped Emma.

"Nice going, Fur-ball," grumbled Charley Crab, rolling his eye stalks.

"Emma." Aunty Pono reached out and touched Emma's cheek. Emma felt a gentle calm settle around her shoulders. "You don't realize how very brave and strong you are, little one," Aunty said. "Listen to the end of the story, and you and I will talk more, all right?" Emma smiled and nodded, and Aunty returned to the Story of the Stones.

"Ignorance is very powerful now," Aunty continued. "He reaches out with a massive swirling cloud arm and wraps his dark smoky fingers around the frightened creatures and people fleeing in the sailing canoe. The strange and terrible thing is that as soon as Ignorance has them in his grasp, they no longer want to leave—because they're empty. Back on Mele Island, they find that all the other creatures and people on the island are empty as well. Some are empty and transparent, with only thin threads of fading fantasies to hold them in place. And some are empty and leaden, with dead eyes focused only on endless repetition and routine.

"But Ignorance isn't satisfied. He knows the power of words, especially *written* words. Ignorance knows those are the most dangerous words of all. They hide in silence and inspire dreams and give shape to dangerous ideas. Ignorance is stronger than before, and he is determined to kill the written word and everything it inspires at the root.

"'Get me the stones!' Ignorance bellows.

"His roar echoes across both islands. It brings despair to almost all who hear it. But one ambitious mongoose longs for the power Ignorance holds and that terrible roar fills him with joy. In a mad dash, the mongoose gets to the stones, grabs the center stone with the eye carved in the top and runs toward Mele Island. But before reaching the shallow water separating the islands, the mongoose trips and falls, and the stone he carries breaks into three pieces with a loud *crack*.

"That *crack* is heard by the three young spirits who put the stones on the island so many years ago. The breaking of one of their stones is a sound they can hear anywhere. The three spirits rush to the islands. They see the mongoose grab the three pieces of the Explore Stone and dash across the Lying Strait and into Ignorance's darkness. Ignorance turns to the spirits and roars, 'These are my islands now! You can't stop me!'

"The three spirits know that Ignorance is partially right, at least about Mele Island. But they also know Ignorance isn't as smart as he thinks he is. The other stones can protect Aloha Island. But the two stones can only keep Ignorance away for so long. Without the center stone, the other two will slowly weaken. The spirits tell the creatures on Aloha Island that one day three children will come to their aid. It is an outlandish promise based on frail hope and faith in the lasting power of words. The spirits promise to stay and use what power they have left to help the remaining two stones keep Ignorance at bay until the three children arrive.

"When they finally arrive, *if* they prove to be brave and strong and curious, they will help the Aloha Islanders get all three pieces of the center stone back, make it whole, and return it to its home. And when that happens, Ignorance will once again be banished, sunlight will pour down on both islands, and Mele Island will sing again."

Eddie, Emma, and Kim looked at each other. Were they the brave, strong, and curious children the Story of the Stones talked about? They couldn't be. Could they?

****

Back at the edge of the forest, Peka Mongoose and the rest of the Flaming Illiterates weren't going to take any chances. They would wait for all these reader nut-bars to go to sleep, and then they would strike first. This time, they would make sure they scared those kids back to wherever they came from, and make sure that they never came back across the Line of Enchantment again.

Chapter 19

Morning Madness

"Code Red! Code Blue! Emergency Purple! Full Alert! Hit the deck! Man the torpedoes!" squeaked a frantic Batbat, as he zoomed and circled in the morning sunlight above Aunty and Uncle's house. "Sabotage! Call the cops! Waaaake uuuup!" he screamed, and he landed on Aunty's kitchen windowsill.

Eddie, Emma, and Kim jumped up from their mats on the lanai as Aunty Pono and Uncle Aka came out of their bedrooms.

"What's all the noise, Batbat?" asked Aunty.

"Are you hurt? Did you have a nightmare? What happened?" asked the kids.

"Look!" said Batbat. He gestured with his little wing to the field and garden behind him.

Aunty, Uncle, and the three kids looked out the kitchen window and couldn't believe their eyes. Like the day before, the sun still poured soft sunlight down from the sweet blue sky above Aloha Island. The distant, proud volcano and the close green trees of the forest still stood strong and tall, but nothing around Aunty's house or Uncle's workshop looked the same at all.

The great living letter garden—rows and rows of carefully tended stalks and trimmed bushes of capital and lowercase consonants and vowels, letter blends and digraphs, punctuation marks, and special words—had been destroyed. Every plant that Aunty had lovingly grown from tiny sprouts had been uprooted and trampled.

"Oh my," Aunty Pono gasped.

There was more. Aunty, Uncle, and the three kids stepped outside and joined Batbat beside the house. Batbat perched on Emma's shoulder as they all slowly looked around. The grass from the field where they sang and had their wonderful Letter Luau last night had been ripped out and thrown all over the place. Aunty's cook pot had been knocked over and had rolled into the tide pool.

"The stones," Uncle said. And the group, now joined by Charley Crab and Ina the I'iwi bird, rushed ahead of Uncle and Aunty to the Old Stones Place.

"Well, they certainly tried to do some damage," said Charley Crab, as Uncle brushed away the dirt and grass strewn around in front of the Old Stones Place.

"The spirits' protection was too strong for whoever did this," Uncle said. "For now, anyway—this is just a slap."

Before Eddie could ask Uncle what he meant, Kim called out from over at the workshop. "Uncle, come quick!" And the whole group of creatures and humans hurried off to see the next bit of disaster visited upon them.

His workshop was pretty badly torn up, but Uncle Aka stayed calm as he looked over the damage. Books, papers, machines, parts, and tools were knocked off shelves, and some of the shelves themselves were torn from the wall. Someone had smashed the big letter funnel flat, and thrown the bright blue hose and massive rainbow sprinkler onto the roof.

"Who would do all this?" asked Kim. "Who could be so mean and destructive?"

Eddie and Emma looked at each other. They knew who could.

"The Flaming Illiterates," they said together.

"The same ones who bat-napped Batbat yesterday?" asked Kim.

"Yes," said Eddie. "But they're not as scary as they think."

"But they are starting to get desperate," said Uncle Aka. "They have never done anything like this before."

Aunty Pono let out a worried sigh, shook her head, and sat in one of Uncle's lawn chairs. "Peka Mongoose, Kolohe Cockroach, and Nunu Pig are not bad creatures, really."

"With all due respect, admiration, and deference, I beg to differ, Aunty," said Charley Crab. Then he began to strut around in a circle with his eyes rolling around dramatically on the ends of their stalks. "Let us look, observe, examine, and yes, inspect what these creatures have done, for Word's sake!" Charley continued, oblivious to everything but his own indignation, the sound of his own voice, and his impressive vocabulary. "As I believe I have previously mentioned to you and to others, not so very long ago, these very same bad-mannered, caustic, vicious, and destructive creatures, if indeed creatures they should be named, came down to our beach, our shoreline, our own shining sand and disrupted, disturbed, and destroyed a very important, significant, and vital meeting of mine. Now, these are bad, wrong, and terrible things they've done. And bad, wrong, and terrible things, I believe, are done by bad, wrong, and…"

Charley didn't notice everyone acting uncomfortable and looking around at anything but him. Everyone but Aunty Pono and Batbat, that is. Batbat was making a frantic pantomime from the roof of the workshop that looked like covering his mouth, locking it, and throwing away the key.

Aunty just looked at Charley. But she was looking at him in *that* way, and her letter lei spelled out *"Shhhh!"* When Charley saw that, his already red shell blushed redder from embarrassment.

"But…um…then again," he said under his breath, as he skittered around looking for a sandy place to disappear, "perhaps first we should hear from Aunty Pono on this matter."

And so they did.

"This gang, the Flaming Illiterates, are silly creatures under the influence of Ignorance. The real bad guy in all this is Ignorance himself," said Aunty. "Ignorance knows the prophecy of the stones, too," she explained. "So he knows that once we have all the stones together again, we'll be too strong for them. And now that he's heard that there are three of you, he'll want to strike us before you have a chance to find the three pieces of the Explore Stone and bring them back."

"Which means we don't have much time," added Uncle Aka.

Eddie looked to Emma and then to Kim. They each took a second, then both looked back to Eddie and nodded yes.

"We're ready," Eddie said. "Just tell us what you need us to do."

Chapter 20

Prisoner of the Dark Atoll

Batbat and Emma helped Aunty pack food and water. Charley Crab ordered sea creatures into units. "Calling all shrimp," he cried out. "Report for duty at the tide pool." Armadas of crustaceans and colorful fish gathered under Charley's commands.

Uncle showed Eddie and Kim a map on his laptop. "As you can see," he said, "much of Aloha Island is unknown territory since the first Ignorance attack. Aunty and I stay close to base to protect the Old Stones Place."

Aunty Pono shook her head. "Are you sure about this, Aka? Maybe the children should stay here with me."

"They'll be safe with me, Aunty," Aka said. "You know that. And, it's been foretold. As a matter of fact, the children are the only ones who are safe."

"Don't worry about us," Eddie said. "We will find the three pieces of stone and we will bring them back."

"We have to tell them about Kanoa, Aka," said Aunty Pono.

A flash of emotion crossed Aka's face. He nodded to Aunty Pono and then stared at his laptop screen.

"Do you want to do it?" Aunty asked Aka. Turning to the children, Aunty said, "She was the love of Uncle's life."

Without looking up from his laptop, Uncle said, "You do it."

"Eddie, Emma, Kim," Aunty said, "there used to be three of us here."

The children looked at each other. Three? Who else?

"For all the time Uncle Aka and I had lived on Aloha Island, we shared our home with a very dear friend," Aunty continued, "a beautiful force of nature named Kanoa (Ka-<u>no</u>-ah, which means *free one* in Hawaiian). Some time ago, after the Explore Stone was stolen, she left on a mission to bring it back. She never returned. We've known and loved Kanoa since…well, I guess, forever. And we still miss her every day. Kanoa thought she could bring back the stone by herself. We told her to wait for the children who were mentioned in the prophecy."

"I begged her to wait until we knew more," said Uncle Aka.

"But she did not have a patient nature," continued Aunty. "She took off in the middle of the night finally. She left a note to Aka saying she was going to sneak onto the Dark Atoll and find the pieces of the stone, even if she had to go toe-to-toe with Ignorance himself."

"Kanoa had a lot of self-confidence," Uncle said, as he gazed over at his workbench. "She stood right over there and told me she'd be back with the stone in a day—two, tops. But," he said, "I never heard from her again." Uncle Aka turned his head aside and brushed away tears.

"Uncle," Kim asked quietly, "is that a picture of Kanoa I saw on your workbench?"

"Yes." Uncle pulled the picture from the drawer where he had hidden it.

"Were you and Kanoa married?" asked Emma.

"In our way, yes, we were," said Uncle Aka.

"Kanoa is being held on the Dark Atoll with all the other people from the old days," Aunty said. "Uncle wanted to go after her, but I knew we had to wait for the children of the prophecy. And here you are."

"Don't worry," said Eddie. "We'll find the pieces of the Explore Stone and Kanoa, too."

"That's right," said Kim. "You wait right here, and we'll take care of everything. Right, Emma?"

"Um, right, yeah," said Emma, who was stealing glances at the dark forest and wondering about the Flaming Illiterates, and people disappearing, and a dark cloud that could grab you with his hand.

"Looks like we've got three Kanoas here," Uncle smiled.

Aunty scooted closer to the kids and put her arm around Emma. "You are all very brave. But you don't think we'd send the three of you off into the woods alone, do you?"

Uncle walked around the workshop and pushed aside a trellis. "I've been working on this invention for a long time, so it would be ready for when you kids showed up."

He opened the door and there sat a tricycle as big as a fire engine. The driver's seat, which was a garden bench with a beach umbrella for shade, was perched in front of a rainbow-colored box filled with bushy green plants. Uncle climbed aboard and pulled out of the garage. Eddie could see "Aloha Island Explorer" painted on the side in bright blue letters. And he could read the letters. Strange. Uncle Aka jumped down from the truck, beaming.

"You're looking at the one and only Aloha Island Explorer," he said. "The only vehicle anywhere powered entirely by spinach!"

Now that prompted all kinds of questions and demonstrations and inspections. The hubbub went on for some time, as the kids were endlessly curious, and Uncle was endlessly proud of his machine, and Aunty Pono was endlessly proud of Uncle.

But Eddie suddenly whistled. "Hey! We've got a magical island to save."

Here's what the kids found out:

Spinach, like all plants, uses energy from the sun to grow. So Uncle figured out a way to turn that energy into electricity to make the truck go. The truck could carry only one passenger, sitting up front with Uncle. Everyone agreed that it should be Emma, because she was the smallest.

Charley Crab and Batbat were coming along because they *really* wanted to. Now everybody bustled about and got this and grabbed that, and told each other what to do like all families do before a big trip. Aunty Pono brought a stack of jelly sandwiches to the truck. She saw Emma sitting over by the Old Stones Place and staring at the forest in the distance. Emma looked up.

"I'm glad Uncle's coming with us," Emma said. "But he can't completely protect us from absolutely everything bad that could happen anywhere on this trip, can he?"

"No," said Aunty. "I'm afraid nobody could do that, Emma. Are you scared?"

"Yeah," sighed Emma. "But I'd be crazy not to be, don't you think?"

"Yes," said Aunty, "you would."

Then the magical Aunty and the brave five-year-old girl smiled at each other, held hands, and walked back toward the rainbow-colored truck with the spinach growing on top, so that Emma could go with Eddie and Kim into the darkest reaches of Aloha Island's forest.

Chapter 21

Prime Minister Rule

"What the heck is that?" whispered Kolohe Cockroach from a hiding spot behind the bushes. He, Nunu Pig, and Peka Mongoose stared at Uncle Aka and Emma sitting up front on the Aloha Island Explorer which rattled along behind Eddie and Kim into the forest.

"Those are pretty colors. It looks kind of like a circus truck. Do you think they've got clowns?" asked Nunu. "I like clowns."

"*You* are the only clown around here," hissed Peka.

This was not what Peka had expected to see after the pounding they'd given Aunty and Uncle's place, and that put Peka on edge. She watched Eddie smile and talk to Kim as they marched through the forest with their circus parade. Even that pompous Charley Crab and that dingbat Batbat, who you'd think would know better after last time, were along for the ride. What were they up to, and what *was* that truck thing? Peka's face scrunched up as she tried to figure it out.

"You like clowns?" Kolohe asked Nunu. "They give me the creeps."

"I used to be scared of clowns, too," said Nunu. "Then my mom told me that their faces weren't really that color. It's just paint."

"I didn't say I was *afraid* of clowns," said Kolohe. "I said they give me the creeps. There's a big difference."

"Would you two put a lid on the clown talk?" barked Peka. "I'm trying to think."

"She's trying to think," Kolohe snickered to Nunu.

"No wonder she's in a bad mood," Nunu snickered back. They ducked as Peka threw a coconut at them. It missed, hitting a tree behind them with a loud *crack*.

****

Emma jumped and scooted closer to Uncle Aka when she heard the loud noise coming from the forest. Uncle Aka smiled and kept driving.

"There's nothing to worry about, Emma. It's just the sounds of plants and animals going about their daily lives in the wild."

"But what if it's the Flaming Illiterates?" Emma asked.

Uncle shrugged. "Could be. But they're not much to worry about. You and Eddie boxed 'em up pretty good last time."

Emma thought that was mostly true, and she really didn't want to seem like a wuss. But the Flaming Illiterates had busted up Aunty and Uncle's place pretty bad. And Aunty and Uncle's friend Kanoa had gone missing, and even if only half of the Story of the Stones was true, there might be a lot to worry about. So, just to be safe, she'd stay close to Uncle or Eddie. Then Uncle stopped the Explorer with a jolt. Right in front of them, in the middle of a clearing, stood a little red guardhouse. It had a black roof, a white-trimmed window in the center of each of its skinny walls, and a yellow-and-black-striped crossing gate stretching across their path.

"What's this?" asked Kim.

"Got me," said Charley Crab, stopping beside her. For once, even he was at a loss for words. Eddie stepped closer to the guardhouse, looking around.

Posted on poles around the guardhouse were very stern, very large, and very official-looking signs. The signs' yellow backgrounds, thick black capital letters, and exclamation points seemed to signal some kind of emergency.

Eddie was too busy trying to absorb the letters and words thrown in front of him all at once to notice much else. He was trying to sound out the big word that started with *A*, when Kim read the whole sign out loud.

"No one allowed beyond this point except letter carriers! All letter carriers must have a carry license at all times!" she read. "Lost carry licenses will be classified as stolen! Stolen carry licenses will be destroyed! Destroyed carry licenses will not be reissued! Reissued carry licenses are invalid! Invalid carry licenses will be destroyed! Destroyed carry licenses will be classified as lost! Anyone without a carry license will be arrested!"

"That doesn't make any sense," Eddie said. He shook his head. "Look at all these signs. Somebody's got a screw loose."

"Or somebody's just trying to scare everybody," said Kim. "Look at what the signs say," she said. She read more of the signs out loud. "Rules are rules! Rules are meant to be *obeyed*! Rule breakers will be arrested! No exceptions! This means *you*! It's for your own good! Don't even *try* it, mister! Don't make me come out there!"

Eddie was getting irritated that Kim read everything aloud before he got a chance to even try. He felt shame slip its hot hand onto the back of his neck like a knowing, nasty bully. Charley sensed what was going on, and tapped on Eddie's foot to get his attention.

"Don't let this jumble of letters and words get to you," Charley said. He pulled out the little book he always carried under his arm and held it up in his claw. "Not so long ago, I was in your shoes. Not literally, of course. I have no use for footwear. Few creatures do. Batbat, perhaps, but that's just for dress-up—make pretend, you know. Now, however, I am the proud author of my own manuscript, tome really, or dare I say it—yes, book. The lesson, my boy, is patience. Be patient, and in time you can do the same."

"Who says I want to?" snapped Eddie. He stepped past Charley, marched up to the little guardhouse, and banged on the door. "Hey! Is anyone here? Open up!" Eddie yelled, and banged on the door again.

"Maybe we should try to be more, you know, polite," Kim said.

"Polite? What's so polite about all these ridiculous signs?"

"*Ridiculous?*" someone squawked from behind the guardhouse door. "There is nothing remotely ridiculous about my signs!" The little red door flew open with a *bang* and standing in front of them was a Nene (nay-nay, which is the Hawaiian goose).

This particular Nene was wearing a tall black-brimmed military hat with a bright gold badge on the front, and he was spitting mad. Kim and Charley edged back as the goose charged forward, flapped his wings, and honked, "You are under arrest! Locked up! Held for questioning!"

Chapter 22

Pinky's Goose Is Cooked

Eddie didn't move an inch and calmly looked the squawking goose in the eye. The goose stopped the racket and looked at Eddie, turning his head this way and that the way geese do, and then puffed out his chest to make sure everybody noticed his black-and-gold sash that matched his hat and had all kinds of impressive-looking medals hanging all over it. "Who *are* you?" the goose asked in that snooty kind of voice that somebody who wants you to go away uses.

"You first," Eddie said.

Kim interrupted, trying to be polite and calm things down. "I'm Kim Kokua, this is Eddie Akamai, and we're visiting from Honolulu, Hawaii, and this is our friend Charley Crab."

The furious bird turned and pulled a rope on the door of the guardhouse with his beak. Out rolled a black-and-gold podium with all kinds of official-looking shields and little flags on it. The goose hopped up and adjusted his big hat. "Who you are and where you come from is of no importance here," he said, trying to make his voice sound deep and dignified. "Rules are important here. Rules make letters and words work. Without rules, they would run around doing whatever they pleased and make a mess out of everything. That is why I, the Prime Minister and Chief Guardian of the Proper Use of Letters, Words, and Sentences, am here. You may address me as Prime—"

Before he could finish, Uncle Aka and Emma came rattling over the hill in the Explorer. Emma hopped out and ran over to Eddie and Kim. When Uncle got out and looked over at the little group by the guardhouse, he shook his head, slapped his knee, and broke out in a big grin. "Pinky?" Uncle Aka said. "Little baby Pinky? Is that *you*?" Uncle Aka ran over and picked up the goose, giving him a big hug. The goose flapped his wings and honked as loud as he could.

"Prime Minister Rule! I am *Prime Minister Rule!*"

Uncle Aka put the flustered Prime Minister Rule back down on his podium, and turned to the others. "A few years ago Aunty Pono and I found an orphaned Nene egg. We cared for the egg until it hatched and raised this little gosling until he was old enough to go out on his own. And now you're a Prime Minister?" said Uncle, turning to the goose. "Your Aunty Pono will be so proud, although, I'm afraid she'll always call you Pinky."

Prime Minister Rule smoothed his feathers, adjusted his hat, and managed a dignified nod in Uncle Aka's direction. "It is good to see you again, Uncle Aka, and do give my regards to Aunty Pono. However, right now I'm afraid I have to attend to my official duties."

"Hey, Pinky, long time no see!" yelled Batbat, as he landed on Emma's shoulder. "Nice hat."

Pinky ignored Batbat. He told everybody that without carry licenses they weren't allowed to go any farther into the forest. There were no carry licenses available because you have to memorize all the rules, and as Prime Minister Rule, Pinky was the only one on Aloha Island that had the rules memorized.

"So," Pinky said, "I hereby order you to go home."

"On whose authority?" demanded Charley Crab.

"Forest authority—*land* authority," answered Pinky. "A *sea* creature wouldn't know anything about it. Also, since you started your question with a preposition, which is a rule violation, you are not allowed to *have* a carry license."

"Listen, birdbrain, no one here cares about your silly rules!" yelled Charley.

"They're not *silly*! They're not even mine!" honked Pinky. "I learned the Rules of Spelling and Proper Usage from Uncle Aka and Aunty Pono!"

The kids, Charley, and Batbat turned to Uncle, who shrugged.

"Well, that's true," Uncle said. "But Pinky, we can't just turn around and go home. See, we're not only gathering and carrying letters, we're helping Eddie, Kim, and Emma find the pieces of the lost Explore Stone, so they can put the pieces back together, put the stone back where it belongs, and save Aloha Island from the forces of Ignorance."

"That's impossible. Can't be done," huffed Pinky. "Besides, that's not my business. I am Prime Minister Rule, and my business is rules."

"What kind of rules?" Emma asked.

"*I* before *E* except after *C* or when it sounds like *A*, like in *neighbor* and *weigh*," honked Pinky, puffing out his chest so his medals jingled.

"Always?" Emma asked.

"Of course! It's a *rule*, isn't it?" snapped Pinky.

"But *weird* is spelled w-e-i-r-d, and *either* is spelled e-i-t-h-e-r," said Kim.

"No, they are *not!*" honked Pinky, flapping his wings.

"Yes, they are," said Kim. "And *height* is spelled h-e-i-g-h-t."

"When two of a word will be fun, just add an *S* and you are done," Pinky honked loudly, ignoring Kim.

"But what about *brush*?" asked Kim. "*Brushes* is spelled b-r-u-s-h-e-s."

"Not true!" squawked Pinky.

"And *baby*?" asked Kim. "If there are two or more babies, change the *y* to an *i* and add *es*. B-a-b-i-e-s."

"No, no, *no!*" insisted Pinky, who jumped around so much on his podium that his sash was backward and his official-looking hat was hanging around his neck by its strap. "*No,* we don't use words that don't obey! *No!*"

"Actually, she's right, Mr. Prime Minister," Uncle Aka said. "There are always exceptions to rules, especially in spelling and grammar."

"Yeah, and that always made you *super* mad, remember?" squeaked Batbat. He chatted on in a happy, friendly way about their school days in Aunty's kitchen. "Remember one time at lunch, you said that if you had your way you'd make all the words follow the rules or kick them out," Batbat said, laughing. "You were so *funny*, Pinky. Like anyone could just decide by himself to make all the rules stick, no matter what. Right, and then what would you do? Go take over some little place in the middle of nowhere and try to *make* everybody do what you say?"

Batbat stopped because everybody was looking at him, except Pinky, whose neck was flushed red from embarrassment. For a minute, nobody knew what to say. Pinky kept his head down, looking at the sash of medals he had made from bottle caps, spray paint, and used ribbons. A big goose tear rolled down his beak and dropped onto the sash.

"I just want words to make sense," Pinky honked. Everybody gathered around Pinky, patted him, and told him not to feel bad.

Everybody except Eddie, that is. Eddie was looking at the words on one of Pinky's signs. He could feel letters and words hooking into his brain and starting to make sense to him. Instead of the letters flipping around on the page to confuse him, they began to move around in a good way—fitting themselves into different parts of his brain and opening up those parts like keys.

Eddie walked away from the group comforting Pinky and ended up on the other side of a stand of paper-bark trees. He liked the quiet. He sat down against a tree, looked at one of Pinky's signs, and tried to sound out the words.

Neither Eddie nor anyone else noticed that reaching from out of the shadows behind the tree were two razor-sharp claws, aiming right for Eddie's neck.

Chapter 23

A Flaming Temptation

Eddie felt the sharp claws on his neck before he saw anything. Just as they began to dig into his skin, he jumped up and swirled around with his fists up. "Who's there?" he demanded.

Peka stuck her head out from behind the tree and smiled. "Don't get all bent out of shape, Eddie. It's just me, Peka Mongoose. You remember me, don't you—forest adventurer and outlaw—leader of the Flaming Illiterates?"

"I remember you, all right," said Eddie, still keeping his fists up.

"Calm down, would you? I'm sorry about kidnapping the bat and all, but we're not such a bad bunch once you get to know us," said Peka. She leaned back against the tree where Eddie had been and crossed her arms.

"What about what you did to Aunty and Uncle's place?" demanded Eddie.

"Yeah," nodded Peka, "that got out of hand. We just wanted to throw you a little scare, but you know how pigs get around a garden full of juicy young letters—nutso. Thing is, I think you and I have a lot in common."

"The heck we do," shot back Eddie. But he lowered his fists.

"Let's just take you, for instance." Counting on her fingers, Peka said, "Smart and unappreciated, hardworking and unappreciated, loyal, generous, and…oh, did I mention unappreciated?" Eddie didn't say anything, so Peka took a step forward and kept talking. "I get the same thing on my side," she said. "Nunu Pig never listens to me, and Kolohe Cockroach thinks he's smarter than I am. Kind of the way your friend Kim acts with you."

Against his better judgment, Eddie found himself sort of agreeing with the smooth-talking mongoose. "So…what do you want?" he asked.

"I thought you and I might be able to find a way to bring the two sides together and work out a kind of peace treaty," Peka said. Then she clapped her paws together and grinned. "Tell you what," she said, taking another step closer to Eddie, "why don't you come with me right now? You can meet the big boss over on Mele Island."

"Are you crazy?" he said. "Go to the *Dark Atoll*?"

"Nobody calls it that except Aunty and Uncle," said Peka. "Come on, Eddie, this is your chance to be a hero."

Just then, Kim's and Uncle's voices filtered through the trees. "Eddie! Eddie, where are you?"

Eddie shook his head. "I don't think so."

"What's the problem, Eddie? I took you to be a brave, take-charge kind of guy," said Peka. "You don't need to get permission from Uncle or Kim, do you? But maybe it's simple, Eddie. Maybe you're just chicken."

At the flash of anger in Eddie's eyes, Peka realized she'd gone one step too far.

"I've got to go," Eddie said, before he turned and walked away.

Kolohe Cockroach and Nunu Pig came out from behind some bushes and stood next to Peka.

"Boy, Peka, you almost had him," said Nunu, as they watched Eddie rejoin his group.

"But then you had to go and call him chicken," Kolohe said. "That was a lame-o move."

"Yeah, it was," Nunu agreed. "Super lame-o. Super lame-o-rama three-D, even."

Peka glared at her two grinning goofball partners. She felt like screaming at the top of her lungs and breaking anything she could find into a million pieces. But even an outlaw mongoose stuck on a magic island with a pig and a cockroach knows that throwing a fit usually only makes matters worse.

****

When Eddie got back to the group, everybody was excited and helping Pinky get settled in the Explorer between Uncle and Emma.

"Pinky's coming with us!" Emma called out happily to Eddie.

"He knows someone who might know someone who knows where the pieces of the stone are," chirped Batbat, as he flew in a circle around the Explorer.

"Or the someone might know where the stones are himself," said Emma.

"I'm not too sure about that part," honked Pinky. "But, I do know he knows something, and he lives down in the Valley of Confusion."

"That part makes sense," added Charley Crab. "Confusion is a perfect place to find a menehune."

"A menehune?" Eddie asked. "Come on, menehune don't exist. They're just made up, like fairies and elves."

Uncle Aka gave Eddie a look. "They exist here, Eddie," he said.

Eddie sighed. "Yeah," he said. "I guess they would."

"Where were you just now, Eddie?" Kim asked. "We couldn't find you anywhere."

"I was taking a break, that's all," Eddie said. "I don't need your permission or anyone else's to do that, Kim, or anything else I want to do."

"Okaaay," Kim said, and shrugged her shoulders. "I was just asking." Then, turning to the Nene, she asked, "Which way do we go?"

So, with Kim and Eddie taking the lead, the group found themselves going down a moss-covered path. The trail switched back and forth around ancient koa trees and huge ferns as it took them farther and farther down into the deep, dark Valley of Confusion.

Chapter 24

The Valley of Confusion

Eddie and Kim had gotten a bit ahead of the others again. Although Charley Crab tried to distract them by pointing out interesting facts (like that they were now in a rainforest, a whole different micro-climate than at the top of the valley), Kim and Eddie were having a "discussion."

Kim asked Eddie where he had been when she and Uncle couldn't find him, and he said, "Nowhere." She asked him what he was doing there, and he said, "Nothing." When Eddie asked Kim why she cared she said, "I don't."

Then they walked around a tight corner where a stream gurgled out from behind a papaya tree. Stepping over the stream, Kim slipped. She would have slid down the slope onto some sharp lava rocks, but Eddie reached out just in time and pulled her back to the path.

"Thanks," Kim said.

"Sure," Eddie said with a shrug. "It's not like I'd let you fall."

Kim smiled. "You wouldn't, would you?"

The two kids looked at each other, and in that split second they both could see that, no matter what, their friendship was a sealed deal.

"So, still friends?" Kim asked.

"Duh," Eddie said.

Then a gentle, laughing voice echoed all around them.

"Well, raise the sword and pass the intuition!" shouted a muscular man around two feet tall with long gray hair and shining eyes who appeared out of nowhere in front of them with a gleaming, sharp machete resting on his shoulder. "All of us were wondering when you two were going to stop fighting like jaybirds," he said.

Neither Eddie nor Kim could do anything but stare at the little man. A soft glow radiated from his deep brown skin that made them feel happy and warm. Then both Eddie and Kim spoke at the same time.

"Are you...are you the menehune?" asked Kim.

"Who's 'all of us'?" asked Eddie.

"Yes," the menehune said to Kim. "My name is Kahiko." (Ka-<u>hee</u>-ko means *old* or *ancient* in Hawaiian.)

"'All of us' means every living thing and spirit in the forest," Kahiko said to Eddie. "We're a large group, and your arguing has been getting on our nerves big-time." Waving for Kim and Eddie to follow, Kahiko turned and started down a path that appeared out of nowhere in the middle of a dense stand of bamboo.

"We're traveling with a group—"

"I know, I know. They'll find you, don't worry," interrupted Kahiko. "Come on."

In a matter of minutes Eddie and Kim found themselves in a leafy, lush clearing, surrounded by a banana tree grove. The rainforest cover opened to the bright blue sky and a golden ribbon of sunlight shone down on a moss-covered stone where Kahiko stood.

Even though they were outside, Kim and Eddie felt like they had stepped into someone's home. There were plenty of comfortable places to sit in the soft grass of the meadow, plenty of bananas and papayas to eat, and fresh water to drink from a stream that ran through the center of the clearing.

As Kahiko had predicted, Uncle, Emma, Charley, Batbat, and Pinky soon arrived in the Explorer. Pinky was relieved that he was right and a menehune did live in the Valley of Confusion. Though Uncle Aka and Kahiko seemed to keep their distance from each other, the rest of the group was excited, and anxious to hear what the menehune had to say. And this was a menehune who loved to talk. Kahiko told them he was very old, centuries and centuries.

As Kahiko talked, he cut the papayas into quarters with his machete. He sliced bananas in half and then in half again, and stuck the banana sails on the papaya quarters with slivers of bamboo.

"I was here way back when the three spirits put the stones on Aloha Island. So I know what was going on." He pointed at Eddie, Emma, and Kim. "You're looking for the three pieces of the Explore Stone." Kahiko connected the two papaya quarters with bamboo and laid a mango leaf across them. "I got all kine magic powers, yeah?" Kahiko said. "But that's not how I knew what you kids were after." Kahiko kept talking, hardly taking any time for a breath as he finished the papaya sailing canoes and handed one to each of his guests. "As soon as Pinky set up his guardhouse, I knew it wouldn't be long before the three children from the prophecy showed up and started poking around."

"But I didn't know anything about it!" Pinky honked, before sticking a banana into his mouth.

"Of course you didn't," said Kahiko. "But everything, all of us, it's all connected, yeah? I could see you were part of big things to come, even though you couldn't. And Eddie, even that tricky mongoose you were talking to today is a part of it. I can't figure out how. But even if I could, I couldn't tell you. Messing with the future is against the rules."

Kahiko winked at Pinky, who broke into a goosey grin. But everybody else was staring at Eddie, who was keeping his head down, not looking back.

"That's why you wouldn't say where you were," Kim said softly, almost to herself, and pulled back from the group.

"A traitor," hissed Charley Crab. "I never thought I'd see the day."

"This isn't true, is it, Eddie?" asked Uncle Aka.

"Of course it isn't!" cried Emma. "You're a liar!" she yelled at Kahiko.

Everybody talked at once. Kahiko sighed and shook his head at his guests. He raised his hand and snapped his fingers, and faster than a fly can flit, a bunch of small dark rain clouds gathered over the group. With a flash of lightning and a clap of thunder, so much rain poured down, it was like the rain was shooting out of the biggest fire hose in the world. Then Kahiko snapped his fingers again, and the clouds vanished. Shocked into silence and soaking wet, everyone looked at Kahiko.

"Holy cow!" Kahiko yelled. "Are all you creatures thick or what? I thought this boy was your friend, your *brudda!*" Kahiko seemed to look everyone in the eye all at once. "Eddie has his journey," Kahiko continued. "He walks it. You got nothing to say about it. The only thing you're in charge of is how *you* act, and just now, that looked *bad*." Kahiko sat down on his moss-covered rock.

"We're sorry," squeaked Batbat.

"From the moment Eddie, Emma, and Kim stepped onto Aloha Island, we *all* became a part of their quest to restore the Explore Stone," Kahiko explained. "All of us have a part to play — doesn't matter we understand, doesn't matter we want to or not. That includes me. And I want *no* part in this — but I got no choice, yeah? Neither do you. So cut all this *out*."

Kahiko looked off into the forest as if he were listening for something. The golden shaft of sunlight returned, and a warm breeze blew through the little clearing, rustling over everyone's wet clothes and hair. No one knew what to say or do, so for a while they just sat there like lumps and watched themselves dry. Then Kahiko stood up and began pacing in a tight little circle.

"Eddie, Kim, Emma, come here," he said. The three kids walked over to him, though Emma, especially, wasn't too happy about it. "If you want to know where the pieces of the stone are, you have to answer a riddle," Kahiko said. "You get one try. If you're right I'll tell you. If you're wrong, you leave Aloha Island immediately and never come back."

"You'd send us home before we found the stone?" asked Kim in disbelief.

"I doubt you'll make it home," said Kahiko. "The forces of Ignorance will probably sink your boat and drown all three of you."

"There's no reason to frighten the little one," Kim said, glaring at Kahiko and putting her arm around Emma, who was getting more scared every minute.

"She doesn't look so little to me," said Kahiko. "She's bigger than I am, and it takes a lot more than a menehune with a riddle to scare me."

"How do we know you know anything, or that the riddle even has an answer?" asked Eddie.

"Because I say so," said Kahiko. "One more thing. The riddle is only for the three of you. One of you has to answer it, and you can't ask any of your friends over there."

"What if we say no?" asked Eddie.

"Then you leave my valley," said Kahiko. "But you never will. It isn't called the Valley of Confusion for nothing. Let's go. Yes or no."

"Kids, don't believe him," called out Uncle Aka. "Menehune are tricksters. You don't have to do it. We'll find another way."

Kahiko shrugged. "You can't have anything if you don't risk everything. But maybe you're just a little too scared to try. We'd all understand. After all, you're only helpless little children," he said.

Eddie looked at the other two. Emma had an even angrier and more determined look on her face than Kim. They nodded at Eddie. He turned back to Kahiko.

"Nobody's scared," Eddie said. "Ask your riddle."

Chapter 25

Short, Mean, and Tricky

Uncle Aka was worried. Under orders from Kahiko, he and Charley, Batbat, and Pinky went to the other side of the meadow. That way they couldn't help Eddie, Kim, and Emma solve the riddle. It's not that Uncle wanted to cheat, but he sure didn't trust Kahiko. Menehune were tricksters, which to Uncle was just another way of saying *liar*, and this menehune had a mean streak. Uncle needed to know what his sister thought they should do.

He wrote an e-mail to Aunty Pono on his computer in the back of the Explorer and sent it to off her.

****

Aunty read Uncle's e-mail and thought for a second. Ina perched on the windowsill and watched her. Aunty Pono took off her letter lei. The letter lei spelled out, "Hey!" and, "What's going on?" Aunty stroked the lei to calm it down, and held it up to Ina the I'iwi bird.

"Ina," she said, "fly as fast as you can to the Valley of Confusion, find the children, and put Letter Lei around Emma's neck. I'm hoping the menehune won't watch Emma as closely as the others."

Ina picked up the lei in her beak and the lei spelled out, "Help!" and, "I'm afraid of heights!"

"Listen up, Letter Lei," Aunty Pono said. "When you get there, you help those kids as best you can. Around Emma's neck, Kim can read you—maybe Eddie, too, a little. And no joking around." Then Aunty clapped her hands. "Go!" she said, and quickly e-mailed her plan to Uncle Aka.

Even more frightened than the lei, Ina flapped furiously and flew off.

****

Back at the meadow, Uncle read Aunty Pono's e-mail and sent Batbat to try and delay the riddle until Ina got there with the letter lei. Luckily, Kahiko loved to talk so much that by the time Batbat dived down to them, he still hadn't gotten around to asking Eddie, Kim, and Emma the riddle.

"So, you see, riddles are tricks, and as you know, we menehune love tricks," said Kahiko. "But riddles are tricks with truth in the middle. Now, the answer to this riddle is one word. And I'll give you one hint—"

"Sorry, sorry, sorry. Don't mean to interrupt, disrupt, interfere, or impede," said Batbat, doing his best Charley Crab impersonation as he landed in front of Kahiko.

"Then flap out of here!" yelled Kahiko.

Batbat was, of course, scared silly. He imitated Charley Crab using tons of synonyms (which are words that mean almost the same thing as one another). "Right away, at once, immediately, Kahiko, sir. But for Word's sake, Uncle Aka is in communication, interaction, or more to the point, consultation, with Aunty Pono, back at her home, abode, or residence, if you will—"

"Get to the point before I chop you in half and turn you into a couple of toads!" yelled Kahiko, as he raised his machete.

"Don't you dare hurt him," warned Eddie.

"No worries, no concerns, Eddie," said Batbat. He turned back to the menehune. "Aunty Pono was curious about your meeting or confab with the three spirits, Kahiko. She's writing a historical book—or tome, if you will—and would like to put your story in a place, position, or station of honor, you see."

Kahiko lit up at this news. "Well, of course, I would like that very much. As I'm sure Aunty Pono is aware, despite the rumors about my present involvement with the disappearance of the Explore Stone, which is blown completely out of proportion, I was standing near the three young spirits when the stones were created. Yes, and it was my idea to set them near the tide pool…"

Out of the blue, Ina the I'iwi bird flew in, dropped the letter lei around Emma's neck, and flew away. Kahiko was still talking about himself so he didn't notice anything.

"They were young spirits, you see," continued Kahiko. "They needed my guiding hand. So that's when I—"

"For Word's sake, look at the time!" interrupted Batbat. "Get us a rough draft—two thousand words, tops, double spaced, no staples, and we'll get back to you. Bye." And like that, Batbat was gone.

"But…but," sputtered Kahiko. Then he shook his head and looked at the kids.

Eddie, Kim, and Emma recognized the letter lei and immediately understood that Batbat's babbling had been a stalling tactic. Now they were petrified that Kahiko would see it around Emma's neck. But just like Aunty Pono predicted, Kahiko didn't notice a thing.

"Where was I?" he asked.

"You were going to give us a hint," said Eddie.

"It's about what you seek," said Kahiko.

"What is?" said Eddie.

"I'm not saying any more," said Kahiko. "Are you ready for the riddle?"

"Is that the hint?" asked Kim.

"Are you ready for the riddle?" Kahiko repeated.

Eddie and Kim nodded.

"Is the menehune really going to make us go back in the ocean and get sunk and drowned and be dead like he said?" asked Emma.

Eddie shushed her and shook his head no. Kim patted Emma's shoulder and shook her head, too. But they both looked plenty worried.

"Listen closely," Kahiko said. "I'll only say it once."

"Go ahead and do it, already," said Eddie. "It can't be that hard."

Kahiko smiled, and then said this:

Pronounced as one letter,
And written with three,
Two letters there are,
And two only in me.
I'm double, I'm single,
I'm black, blue, and gray,
I'm read from both ends,
And the same either way,
What am I? †

All three kids looked at each other, their lips moving as they silently repeated the riddle to themselves so as not to forget it. Emma thought Eddie and Kim looked even *more* worried now.

Kahiko stretched and yawned. "I'm going to take a nap," he said. "You have until sundown to come up with the answer." Kahiko glanced at the sun lowering in the purple late afternoon sky. "That doesn't give you much time," he said, and then grinned at Emma. "Looks like you'll be back out in the ocean real soon."

"We'll have the answer in one minute!" Emma yelled at Kahiko as he walked away, and then crossed her eyes and stuck her tongue out at him.

When Eddie and Kim looked at the letter lei around Emma's neck, they looked even more worried than Emma had ever seen them. Because for once in its short, smart-alecky life, the letter lei had nothing to say.

Chapter 26

Emma and the Bee

Spirit; no. Stone, piece; no and no. Old, seeker, man, god; no, no, no, no. Eddie, Kim, and Emma kept throwing words back and forth, thinking anything to match the riddle. If it had to do with the stone, it had to be something they knew, or had heard of. The sun kept going down, and the more they tried to think, the more their brains seemed to freeze.

And even worse, their ace in the hole, the letter lei, was acting like it didn't know any words at all. It didn't even throw out any smart-aleck joke to ease the tension. Of course, the kids didn't know that Aunty Pono had told the lei, "No jokes!" And the lei wasn't about to cross Aunty on that, especially since it couldn't come up with the answer, either.

Emma noticed that Eddie and Kim tried to beat each other to the right answer and were always the first to put the other one's answer down. This made things even more tense, which made Emma wish that somehow the answer would appear in the sky or something, since the loser letter lei wasn't any help, and she really didn't want to drown or be eaten by sharks or zapped by dark forces or whatever.

Now, the thing about the letter lei was that the budding letters in it were very fragrant, especially the vowels. Those wonderful smells sometimes attracted bees, and one was buzzing around Emma's neck, trying to land on a pretty blue *I*. Emma tried brushing it away, but the bee was determined.

"Get away from the *I*, will you?" she mumbled.

"Emma, be quiet. We're trying to think," Eddie said.

Emma took another swipe at the bee, and it dodged her hand and bounced against her face. Emma giggled. "This bee keeps going at the little blue letter *I* and then almost flies into my…*oh!*" At the top of her voice, Emma yelled, "That's it! Eye! The symbol on the stone is an eye! And the answer to the riddle is an *eye!*"

And, of course, that's exactly what it was. Everybody cheered and jumped up and down. Uncle ran over and gave them all big hugs, Pinky honked, Charley skittered around, and Batbat flew in big backward loops above their heads. The kids were surprised to see that even Kahiko seemed happy for them. He told them that the next morning they'd go down into the valley the rest of the way until they reached Teach Beach. There, they would find Jay and Kay, the rhyming dolphin twins, who would help them find the first piece of the stone.

But before all that, Kahiko was going to have a luau for the group with some of his friends, and after the luau they'd have a more serious talk. There was more to the Story of the Stones than they had heard so far. They had to learn the rules.

That figures, Eddie thought. Every time kids start to get good at something, grown-ups throw in more rules.

****

That night's luau was even more unusual than the Letter Luau at Aunty Pono and Uncle Aka's place. All kinds of different forest animals came, even ones that normally spent their time trying to eat each other, because Kahiko called a temporary truce for the luau. So Maestro Owl shared his dish of poi with a mouse, and the happy face spider and a couple of flies sat next to each other eating a mango salad. Later, the spider asked the flies if they wanted to go see his cool web design, but they could tell what he was planning behind that happy face, so they told him to buzz off. Finally the night came to an end, and as he was leaving, Maestro Owl, who turned out to be as smart as an owl is supposed to be, congratulated Emma on answering the riddle.

"It takes a calm mind like yours to look for possibilities instead of answers," he said.

After all the forest creatures had left, Kahiko sat down with the group. "All right," he said, "before we go down to Teach Beach in the morning, you all should probably hear the part of the Story of the Stones that even you don't know about, Uncle Aka. I think you'll find it interesting."

Interesting? Uncle Aka thought that what Kahiko told them next was horrifying.

Chapter 27

These Boxes Bite

Kahiko said that back in the old days, when the Story of the Stones wasn't a dusty old story but was real, everyday life, he had a sit-down with the big man of the dark forces, Ignorance himself, along with his henchmen, Fear and Apathy.

"All three are foul, huge, and dark spirits, with long greasy talons instead of hands and gaping holes in their faces dripping with fungus and decay instead of mouths. So, yeah, their breath just about knocks you down with the terrible smell of the rotting hopes and dreams of thousands of souls. But, hey, I figured I was smarter and trickier than them, so no worries, right?" Kahiko looked at Uncle Aka. "That was my first mistake," Kahiko said.

It turned out, Ignorance, Fear, and Apathy tricked Kahiko the menehune, instead of the other way around.

They told him they had some very vicious vapors even they couldn't control that needed to be locked up in a way so nobody could let them out. So Kahiko made them three magic boxes with magical locks that could be opened only with correct answers to very difficult riddles. And then he helped them hide the boxes.

"I think what they really put in the boxes were the three pieces of the Explore Stone," Kahiko said. "My conscience has been bugging me for a few hundred years. So when the rumor went around that the three kids from the prophecy were finally coming, I thought it might be my chance to rectify things." He looked at Eddie, Emma, and Kim. "I had to find out if you were the real thing first, of course. It seems like you are. So, get your rest. Tomorrow you'll start the really hard part of your adventure."

****

The next morning, the letter lei swinging from her neck, Emma walked in front, leading the Explorer with Kim, Eddie, and Kahiko. Emma felt more grown-up than she had ever felt before.

Kahiko seemed even more serious than last night, if that was possible. He explained one more thing about the lost pieces of the Explore Stone and the magic boxes they were hidden in. "Ignorance and his two creepy friends hate the stones, of course. As you know, the stones have great power. When they're together they can obliterate Ignorance, Fear, and Apathy."

"Then why didn't the bad guys throw the pieces of the Explore Stone into the ocean or something?" asked Emma.

"Yeah," said Kim, "why bother with the boxes and stuff?"

"Good question, girls," said Kahiko. "You have any ideas on that, Eddie?"

Eddie shook his head.

"Well, Ignorance and his bunch would have thrown the pieces of the Explore Stone into the ocean if they could have. But unless the pieces of the broken stone are kept apart, they are drawn together. Magic boxes with magical locks were the perfect solution to keep all three from reuniting. I played right into it. They just needed someone to make the boxes for them." As he was talking,

Kahiko led them around a bend, and the wide-open blue sky and bright white sand of Teach Beach stretched out before them.

"So all you have to do is show us where the boxes are, tell us the answers to the riddles and we're home free, right? It doesn't sound like that much of a challenge," Eddie said.

Kahiko laughed. "What part of 'magical' don't you understand, boy?"

Eddie shrugged. Kim knew how much Eddie didn't like being laughed at.

"Kahiko, come on," Kim began.

Eddie interrupted, "It's OK, Kim." He then turned back to Kahiko. "There's a lot I don't understand, Kahiko. I'm a kid."

"Good point," Kahiko said. "OK, it's like this. These aren't cute little wooden boxes for your sparkly keepsakes, or shoe boxes, or any kind of boxes you're familiar with. These boxes are alive."

"Alive in what way?" asked Kim.

"Alive in like they can bite your hand off," said Kahiko. "Once I laced the spell through them, they started breathing, thinking, and moving around on their own. They can't go too far. They are boxes, after all. But they squirm around and burrow to stay hidden."

By this time they were all standing in the middle of the longest and prettiest beach any of the kids had ever seen. And they grew up in Hawaii, so that's saying something. Kim looked out at the water. Perfect six-foot waves were rolling in, one after the other. She wished she had her surfboard. Uncle parked the Explorer and walked over with Ina, Pinky, Charley, and Batbat to join them.

"Just in time to hear the last bit about the magic boxes, Uncle Aka," said Kahiko. "This is the most wonderfully demented part of the spell, if I do say so myself. Once they had their treasures to guard, the boxes made up their own riddles. I don't know the answers, Eddie. I don't even know the questions. Now here's the truly twisted part." Kahiko chuckled in admiration of his own genius. "I've got to say, if you hire me to protect your stuff it will be protected in spades," he said.

"Get to it, Kahiko," said Uncle Aka.

"All right," said Kahiko. "It's this. If you manage to find one of the magic boxes, and then manage to hold on to it long enough for the box to ask you the riddle—and they do not like being held—then you have one chance and one chance only to answer the riddle and retrieve your prize."

"What happens if you guess wrong?" asked Emma.

"You'll like this," said Kahiko, "or maybe you won't, but you'll have to appreciate the genius of it."

"Enough, Kahiko," said Uncle.

"The box dies," Kahiko said. "And then, in a matter of seconds, it decomposes and dries into the size of a kukui nut. And what about the prize trapped within the box?" Kahiko asked. He looked from face to face, enjoying the moment. "Whatever the prize inside the box was, even if it was, say, a very powerful and magical stone, it is crushed into complete and irretrievable nothingness. It's gone, for forever and ever." Kahiko winked at Eddie. "Is that enough of a challenge for you, boy?"

Chapter 28

Peka Makes a Move

Uncle Aka's expression darkened. "So," he said to Kahiko, "you're proud of what you've done?"

"Purely as a craftsman, Uncle," said Kahiko. "You have to understand, after the last big attack some of us felt that it was only a matter of time before that bunch took over anyway."

Eddie, Kim, and Emma had never seen Uncle Aka even close to angry. But he was angry now, his eyes burning with a terrible cold fire.

"Kanoa, a friend I love and value beyond measure, disappeared searching for the stones," Uncle said.

"I swear I didn't talk to her, didn't even see her out here," Kahiko said.

Uncle took a long breath, and held his temper. "Why should we trust you after what you've done?" he said.

"I'm on your side, now. If you don't want my help, that's fine with me," Kahiko said.

The menehune turned back toward the Valley of Confusion, but Emma stepped in his path.

"You said you felt bad about what you did," Emma said. "You said you'd help fix it."

Kahiko looked up at the sky. Then he pointed out at the water. "See those two dolphins?" he said.

Everybody looked, and two dolphins appeared, jumping into a wave and riding it down to the break. Then they flew out of the foam and swam back toward the swells.

"Those are Jay and Kay, the Rhyming Dolphin Twins," Kahiko said. "Rumor has it they know where one of the boxes is. Only they won't talk to anybody who doesn't surf with them. Any of you kids a surfer?"

"Kim's a great surfer," Eddie said.

"But I don't have a board," Kim said.

Kahiko grinned. "Over in the bushes near the end of the path there's an old long board I use sometimes."

"I'll get it for you," said Eddie, and he ran back up toward the bushes.

After Eddie took off, Ina told Uncle she was heading back to Aunty Pono to update her on all the news. Ina planned to take the letter lei back with her, but the lei wanted to "hang around" Emma for a while, so Ina was going back solo.

****

Peka, Nunu, and Kolohe crouched behind the bushes near the beach.

"I told you he was ready to ditch that bunch," Peka said. "All we had to do is be in the right place at the right time."

"I'll believe it when I see him on the Dark Atoll," said Kolohe.

"No one calls it that," snapped Peka.

"Yes, they do. Everybody does," said Nunu.

"Lid...on...*it*!" hissed Peka.

Eddie was just a few feet away and approaching the bushes. He pushed the bushes aside and came face-to-face with the Flaming Illiterates.

"What are you doing here?" Eddie said.

"Eddie, my man!" crowed Peka. "It's good to see you finally found the courage to leave those reading bozos behind. Come on, the big man is anxious to meet the famous Eddie and welcome you to the No Reading, No Writing Zone."

Eddie leaned closer to the Flaming Illiterates. "I used to think like you guys. But since I came to Aloha Island, things look, well, different."

"Don't fall for it, Eddie. Reading and writing are glue traps for losers," Peka said. "Use your eyes—they study-study-study all day long in her tiny kitchen filled with potted letter flower plants they're not allowed to eat. What do we do? We put our feet up and relax in sun-drenched comfort."

"Where?" asked Eddie.

"What?" said Peka.

"Where do you relax in sun-drenched comfort?" asked Eddie.

"The dump," said Peka. "Where else?"

"It's a real 'guy' kind of place," said Nunu, "easygoing, no aunties around yapping at you to pick things up."

Peka turned back to Eddie. "The best part is: no studying, reading, or writing. Most days we don't even think."

"You should come," said Kolohe Cockroach. "I found a whole stack of old boxing magazines when I was nosing around for a snack the other day. You can have 'em. You like boxing? Humans like boxing, right?"

Eddie looked at the once-feared Flaming Illiterates. He shook his head. "I gotta go, guys," he said.

"Eddie, wait, don't go!" Peka yelled after him. "The big man really wants to see you!"

As Eddie carried the surfboard down to Kim, he heard arguing coming out of the bushes, and then the hollow *bonk* of a pig being beaned with a coconut.

****

Kim was stoked. She had never been on such a long ride on such a perfect wave in her entire life. And she was riding in the company of two friendly dolphins who really knew their way around a wave.

"We play in the spray all day," said Jay.

"We look the same, but don't share a name," explained Kay, as she zoomed down the wave beside Kim.

"And we play our game," said Jay, on Kim's other side, "but we're not tame, don't jump through hoops for fame, that's not why we came."

They flipped over the back of the wave as it broke, and Kim followed.

"Jay and Kay," Kahiko yelled from the beach, "you might be able to help us. Do you know where any of the boxes are?"

The dolphins glanced at each other and laughed the high dolphin cackle. Then they dove down into the water. Kim wondered if she could breathe under water on this side of the island and without Uncle Aka with her. *Well,* she thought, *there's one way to find out.* Kim waved to Eddie on the beach, pushed Kahiko's surfboard toward shore, and dove in after the dolphins.

Kim followed Jay and Kay down to a long, wide reef. She was happy to realize she was breathing the water just like she did way back at the Switcheroo Championship.

The two dolphins led her deeper, toward a trough in the seafloor. Kim could feel the fear rising inside her, but she fought it down. Everybody was counting on them. She had to do her part. Besides, it couldn't be much farther. The dolphins would stop any second.

But they didn't. They kept leading her farther down and then into the trough, which was lined with jagged rocks and pale, stringy sea plants that reached out at her as she swam by. And now it wasn't just deep, it was cold, too. And it was getting very dark.

Chapter 29

Ina Hangs

"*Eee–eee-vee!* Torture! *Eee!* Help, Aunty Pono! *Eee-eee-eee!* Murder!" screeched Ina.

"Oh, for pity's sake, put a lid on it, bird," said Peka. "Aunty Pono can't hear you."

But little red Ina the I'iwi bird was in a complete panic and kept screeching like crazy. She'd never been caught by anyone ever before, but the Flaming Illiterates had seen her take off from the beach, and had run ahead and strung a super-fine fishing net in her flight path. With her head so full of worries and responsibilities, Ina had flown right into it. Now, these horrible beasts had her tiny feet tied with morning glory vine and she was hanging upside down from the branch of a monkey-pod tree. No matter how hard she flapped her little red wings, she couldn't get upright. Consequently, on top of being petrified, she felt like she was going to throw up. Ina hated even the idea of throwing up, because it was icky and slimy and reminded her that she sometimes ate bugs.

"*Eee-eee-vee! Help!* Aunty Pono will *get you! Eee!*" shrieked Ina.

"Ow, my ears," said Nunu.

"Yeah, she sounds like a rusty hinge," said Kolohe. "You'd think a bird that ate honey would have a sweeter-sounding voice."

"*Eee-eee-vee!*" screeched Ina.

Peka grabbed Ina's long beak in her paw and got eye to eye with the trembling little bird. "Listen to me, you pip-squeak," said Peka. "The whole island knows what a gossip you are. We just want you to share some of it with us. You do that, we'll let you go, mongoose honor."

Nunu and Kolohe burst out laughing.

"Pay no attention to them, Ina. I'm the boss. I'm going to let go of your beak, you'll talk, and then I'll let you leave. Ready?"

Ina nodded. Now that she understood they weren't going to pluck her and roast her for lunch, she felt better. Plus, she liked having information they wanted. Also, p.s., and by the way, Ina considered herself a champion gossip and her firsthand account of being kidnapped by the Flaming Illiterates could be number one with a bullet on the gossip charts across Aloha Island, from tree to sea.

So when Peka let go, Ina told them what had happened with the kids and Kahiko the menehune. At first she tried to be like a spy and leave out little pieces of what happened. But that was way too complicated and gave Ina a headache. She was hanging upside down, after all. So in the end, Ina spilled her birdie guts, Peka cut the vine, and Ina flew home as fast as she could.

As she flew home, Ina decided she wasn't all that concerned about what she had done. Not everyone was cut out to be a hero. Maybe she shouldn't have told, but she was sure Aunty Pono and Uncle Aka could handle anything that the bad guys might do. There was nothing to worry about. When she got back to Aunty Pono's house, all Ina would have to do was adjust her story a little bit.

****

Ina was right; not everyone was cut out to be a hero. Heroes were rare. About the time Peka had cut Ina loose, one would-be hero, Kim, was deep in the ocean in a very dark, cold, and scary trough in the seafloor. Jay and Kay, the dolphin twins, were guiding her up to the edge of a small hole in the sharp rocks.

"Lucky thing your hands are thin, because now it's time to reach on in," the twin dolphins said in unison.

Obviously Kim was brave. She had just swum down to a narrow rocky crevice in the bottom of the ocean with a couple of rhyming dolphins she barely knew, and she hadn't made a peep. But she knew better than to stick her hand into dark, unexplored places under water. Moray eels, scorpion fish, and other dangerous creatures lurked in places like that.

The dolphins saw her hesitate, and Jay immediately said, "Oh, we forgot one thing, but don't be sad, when we make this sound, the bad get mad."

Then Kay told her to cover her ears. Kim did, and the twin dolphins got close to the hole in the rocks and let go with a double-barreled dolphin squeal that made the whole rocky crevice shake. Then *bang!* Two moray eels and a scorpion fish flew out of the hole in the rocks, screaming in pain, and swam away as far and as fast as they could.

"Those guards for Ignorance left for today, but now you make them stay away," Jay said.

Kim knew that meant it was her turn. She swam close to the hole and peered in. She could see a shape about the size of a shoe box in the back corner of the rock shelf. She slowly reached in with both hands. Then suddenly there was movement. It was the box. The box was moving. This was creepy. But Kim stuffed the fear down again, and with one quick move she shoved herself into the dark hole and grabbed for the squirming box that was disappearing farther into the dark.

Kim nabbed the squirming box, and pulled it out of the hole. With Jay and Kay on either side of her, she swam for the surface. When they got close to the beach, Kim thanked the twins for their help. As the dolphins swam back to their perfect waves, Kim gripped the box tightly and walked toward the beach.

The whole excited group came running up to her. Kim held the box out toward the others. "This," Kim said, "is—no contest—the ickiest, creepiest, most disgusting thing I have ever touched in my entire life."

Chapter 30

Now It Begins

"Eee! No!" Ina screeched. "I will tell you nothing, Peka Mongoose, no matter what you do to me! I am a soldier!"

Aunty Pono sat at her kitchen table shelling baby *p*'s and listening to Ina's story, thinking that this bird had to be the worst liar she had ever heard.

"If you have any information you did not get it from me! I am no talker!" Ina growled, staring across the sink at an imaginary Peka.

Though Ina didn't know that much, Aunty knew that Ignorance had learned from Ina that the three children from the prophecy were here and they were going after the pieces of the Explore Stone. Knowing this, Ignorance and his whole army would come to stop them, and soon. Aunty smelled trouble.

"I am loyal and strong—not disloyal and weak, like you!" Ina crowed. She jumped across the sink and pecked at a sponge. "Take that!"

Aunty had to get word to Uncle Aka and the kids, and obviously couldn't use Ina. And now that Ignorance had been tipped off he'd go after her and Uncle Aka's e-mails, looking for more information. Not being able to read wouldn't stop him; he'd use some poor empty shell of a human on the Dark Atoll to read the e-mails for him. It was clear that from now on, any communication with Uncle, Eddie, Kim, or Emma would have to be face-to-face. Aunty put down the *p*'s. It was time to get organized.

"Go ahead and beg, mongoose," Ina said. "It does you no good!" She threw the sponge in the air and screeched in victory.

"Stop that," Aunty said, as she stood up from the table.

Ina froze. The sponge fell to the floor with a wet *plop*.

"I want you to gather Hazel and all the rest of your gossipy friends, and tell them I want the loyal land and sea creatures in our area to meet me at the tide pools in fifteen minutes. We're rolling."

****

Eddie, Kim, and Emma, wearing the letter lei around her neck, sat on the sand with the brown riddle box. Kahiko and the rest of the group waited down the beach, out of earshot, and watched the kids.

The three watched the box as it squirmed around in the sand, making impatient little clicking sounds. It was slimy like a slug, but Kim said the skin felt thick and strong, like a lizard's. There was no latch, lock, edge, or any hint of an opening, except for the tiny mouth on one end of the box making the clicking noises.

Kim said, "Look, you can see the teeth clicking together in there."

Emma scrunched down to look. "Eeew," she said. "They're like little rat teeth."

"So, guys?" Eddie asked. "Time to give it a shot?"

Eddie and Emma agreed Kim should be the "handler" for the first box, since she was the one who found it. She did as Kahiko had told them and put both hands on the slimy skin of the box. She took a deep breath to calm herself, and as she did, Kahiko's last instructions rang in her head.

"The box only listens to the handler, the one whose hands hold it and who asks for the riddle," Kahiko had told them. "The handler must keep both hands on the box until the riddle is answered. You three can talk and guess until you have your answer. Then whichever one of you is the handler must say, 'Box, we have the key,' and give your answer. If you're right, you get your piece of stone. If you're wrong, or if either of the handler's hands leaves the box before the answer's given—well, you know. Aloha Island is history."

Not too much pressure, thought Kim. And then she asked the question rhyme that Kahiko had taught them. "Box, I wish to open your locks," Kim said. "I can answer your riddle, I'm crazy like a fox."

The box snapped its teeth together with a loud *clack*. A moment passed without a sound, and then, as all three kids bent closer to the box, it began to slowly open its dark little lizard-skinned mouth.

Chapter 31

One Down

With all three of the kids almost shaking from anticipation, the ugly little bread-loaf-shaped box spoke. And in a surprisingly sweet voice, the box gave them this riddle:

> *Here on the beach you can say,*
> *Yesterday is always before today;*
> *But there is a place where yesterday*
> *Always follows today.*
> *Where?* †

Then the box sighed and snuggled against Kim's hands, and an odd wave of tenderness for the magical box crept over her.

"The moon?" said Emma.

"What?" said Eddie.

Emma raised her eyebrows and pointed to her lei, which spelled out *moon* plain as day.

"Moon." I just read that word right off the lei, thought Eddie. I'll show Kim and Kumu and everyone else. I'll be the best reader anywhere. They'll have to admit it to my face, and it won't be long. Who am I kidding? I can say I'm going to be some great reader to everyone else, even Kim—especially Kim. But inside my head there's no fooling me. Sometimes the same letters I read one minute look totally different the next. Oh, man, if Kim knew what a moron I really am...

"Eddie!" Kim's voice snapped him out of his head.

"Yeah?" said Eddie.

"Any ideas?" said Kim.

"Why couldn't it be the moon?" asked Emma again. "It's far away, and maybe the days do go backward there. You don't know."

"I do know," said Eddie. "The moon goes around the earth and the earth goes around the sun, so they're both going the same way in time — which, last time I checked, is forward."

"If they're going around, they're not going forward, they're going back to the same place," Emma said.

"So?" Eddie said. "I was talking about time."

"So," Emma said, "up on the moon time could be different."

"Emma, Eddie, this isn't helping," said Kim. "It's not the moon. But remember Kahiko's riddle, which you solved, Emma. We have to listen to all of what the riddle says, and let it sink in."

So they sat and thought very seriously, over and over, *Where does yesterday follow today?*

Though she tried very hard not to, Emma kept imagining the moon as a place where everything went backward. Clocks went backward, calendars went backward. People even walked backward.

All Kim could think was that maybe there was a foreign country that didn't believe what every other country believed. Was there a whole country of contrary people who decided that yesterday and today were in the wrong order? This didn't seem likely.

When Eddie wasn't arguing with himself in his head, he was arguing with his sister. But right at this second, Eddie's brain was in a rage because nobody, not even he himself, thought he had any brains. Take away the reading, he was a smart guy. But even his five-year-old sister thought she knew more about the moon than he did. The moon that his dad had taught him controls the tides; the moon with its dependable, predictable phases, always moving forward.

I mean, come on. Yeah, she's only five, but does Emma seriously think that there are people on the airless moon living life in reverse? Clocks backward, calendars backward, walking backward, talking backward, reading backward. The dictionary would have to be in reverse… Wait. That's it.

Eddie looked up and immediately was eye to eye with Emma, who also had a huge grin on her face. Laughing, they yelled to Kim at the same time, "The dictionary! Yesterday always follows today in the dictionary!" Then they rolled around on the sand laughing.

OK, thought Kim, the Akamai kids have cracked under the pressure.

But Eddie and Emma managed to pull themselves together in time to convince Kim that "the dictionary" really was the answer. So, Eddie and Emma sat close to Kim again, who still held the magic box in both hands.

Kim took a deep breath and said, "Box, we have the key…the dictionary."

And that's when things got weird.

Chapter 32

Driving with Dinosaurs

The box squirmed out of Kim's hands, fell to the sand, and rolled over on its side with an angry hiss. "You are correct," it snarled. It shook all over like a rattlesnake's tail. It groaned and moaned. It blew up like a puffer fish. Then its tiny mouth and teeth grew into a gaping ugly hole.

Just when all three kids were about to run for the hills, the box let out the heaviest sigh any of them had ever heard and an enormous tongue rolled out of its mouth and plopped on the sand. Sitting in the middle of the soft red velvet tongue was what looked like the first piece of the Explore Stone. Kim carefully reached out and snapped up the piece of stone, and brought it over to Uncle.

"You've done it, kids" he said, and grinned from ear to ear. "This piece is the real thing, the middle one of the three pieces of the Explore Stone."

The kids laughed and congratulated each other, and the creatures jumped around celebrating, but Kahiko interrupted their merriment.

"This is just one piece. You've got to find the other two," he said.

"OK, where do we go?" Eddie said.

"Go through the forest to the other side of the volcano. Some paniolos (pan-ee-oh-lohs, which means *cowboys* in Hawaiian) had a ranch up that way before the attack by the forces of Ignorance sucked them onto the Dark Atoll." Only creatures lived on the ranch now, but Kahiko said one of them, a pony named Punk, might know where the second magic box was.

So, without stopping to rest, the kids, Uncle Aka, and their band of creatures gathered around the Explorer and prepared to head out. Just as Emma asked, "Aren't you coming with us?" the menehune vanished.

So the group headed up the volcano road into the thick forest. Kim and Eddie walked ahead of the Explorer, and Batbat flew scout, squeaking, "All clear!" and, "Bad guys beware!" at frequent intervals. Uncle and Emma rode up front like before, except this time, to her delight and Charley Crab's horror, Emma got to drive.

"You cannot allow a child to operate, drive, or otherwise control this vehicle!" Charley yelled from the back cargo compartment he shared with Pinky the Nene, who had been immediately rocked to sleep when the Explorer started up the road.

"Why not?" Uncle said.

"Why not, you ask? Safety, Uncle, that's why not," said Charley. "But maybe this excursion isn't dangerous enough for you. Maybe chasing after creepy enchanted boxes with teeth right under Ignorance's evil nose is so boring that you have to spice things up by putting us all at the mercy of an untrained, untaught, unqualified, underage driver. Was that the idea?" Charley turned to Emma. "No offense, Emma. I'm simply trying to understand."

Emma wasn't offended. She never paid much attention to anything Charley said anyway. Who could? He was always talking in circles. So she just looked back at him with a smile and said, "Whatever."

"Keep your eyes on the road!" Charley screeched.

"Oh, for Word's sake, Charley," Uncle said. "The Explorer can only go four or five miles per hour. How much trouble can Emma get into?"

Charley rolled his eye stalks and finally gave up. Uncle opened his laptop computer and started typing in his daily journal, which he always started with *"Dear Kanoa."*

Grumbling to himself, Charley Crab sat back down next to the napping Nene and reached for the one thing that always made him feel better—a thesaurus. When he pulled the heavy book off the shelf, it bumped against Pinky's leg and woke him up.

"Hey!" Pinky honked, darting his head all around. "Who's there? What's that?"

"Calm down," Charley said. "It's just my thesaurus."

"You have a dinosaur in here?" yelled Pinky. "Help!"

"No, no, no," said Charley. "A thesaurus. It is a book filled with words and their synonyms."

"Well," said Pinky, still glancing around to make sure that some allosaurus-like dinosaur wasn't going to jump out and bite him, "I don't know what 'nyms' are, but I do know 'sins' are bad things. You better put that book away before Uncle sees it."

Being, he thought, a patient, generous and good-hearted crab, Charley carefully explained what a synonym was—a word that meant almost the same thing as another word.

"Oh," said Pinky. "*That's* where you get all those words you jam together. Why do you do that, anyway? To try and make yourself sound smart?"

Charley was so shocked that his eye stalks stood up straight and vibrated like tuning forks. That anybody at all would say such a thing to him was bad enough. But to hear it from a fat bird who wore homemade bottle-cap medals, Charley thought, was more than any self-respecting crab could bear.

"Ah...ah...," Charley said, and then, "uurp."

"I was just asking," Pinky said, and went back to sleep, leaving Charley sitting in front of his thesaurus, too upset to speak.

Uncle overheard Charley and Pinky and wrote about it in his journal.

Even if he had been able to calm down enough to answer Pinky, Charley couldn't have said why he likes using all those synonyms, Uncle wrote. Maybe it's to impress other creatures, or maybe he just likes the sound of all the words jammed together, fighting for space—he really doesn't know for sure. But I don't think most of us really know the reasons why we do the things we do. In the end, we are all mysterious creatures with mysterious brains. That's it for today, Kanoa. As always I pray that you are safe, and I live only for the day I see your face again.

Uncle closed the laptop. He saw the sunlight float through the trees and felt the gentle breeze as Emma guided the Explorer up the forest road. "What a good driver you are," Uncle told her.

"Thanks," Emma said. "But my arms sure are getting tired."

"Pull over. It sounds like it's my turn at the wheel," Uncle said.

Then, just as Emma pulled over, and Uncle was about to step down off the Explorer, a loud *crash* stopped him cold. Something huge and loud was smashing through the trees, and it was coming right at them.

Chapter 33

The Unstoppable Bull

All Emma could think was thank goodness she'd pulled over. Because with another thundering *crash*, a humongous black bull exploded onto the path where the Explorer would have been if they hadn't just stopped. Then a pinto pony wearing a straw cowboy hat, with its ears sticking out through the hat's brim, came barreling through the bushes after the bull.

"Comma! Period! Capital letter!" shouted the pony. "New paragraph!"

But the bull paid no attention and ducked behind the Explorer, and the pony chased him around and around the vehicle. Uncle, Emma, Charley, Pinky, and the letter lei were trapped in the Explorer by the circling animals. The Explorer shook so much from the pounding hooves that the vowel cart fell over in the cargo area, almost landing on top of Pinky, who woke up yelling, "Dinosaurs!" Charley, meanwhile, ran back and forth trying to keep the books from falling off the shelves, and up on the roof of the Explorer the spinach plants were shaking loose and raining down around everybody.

Holding on to her seat with both hands to keep from falling off, Emma noticed she wasn't nearly as scared as she had been on the ocean. She didn't know what that meant, exactly, but she liked it. She also noticed the bull was talking nonstop as he pounded around and around the Explorer.

"The last thing I wanted was to eat and run," the bull said, his words tumbling on top of each other in a jumble. "But how could I help it when all around me in every corner certain creatures, and I don't mean all, but the ones that were concerned, not the ones who were not concerned or the ones who couldn't concern themselves with that concern…"

The pony, trying to trick the bull and cut him off, suddenly reversed direction, and came around the other side. But the bull sensed the change, feinted left, broke right, and was off running up the volcano road.

The pony chased after him, yelling, "Period, dagnabbit! *Period*, you big galoot!"

Eddie and Kim, who were hurrying back to see what the trouble was, jumped out of the way of the bull and pony, and then ran back to the Explorer.

"Follow that pony!" Eddie shouted.

Chapter 34

Book 'Em, Eddie

The troop chased after the pony and the bull. While Eddie and Kim raced ahead, the Explorer chugged along to keep up. Around one bend, then another, and finally there was the pony they could only assume was Punk, putting the rebellious bull back into his corral.

Sure enough, it was. Punk told them her name was short for Punctuation, which was her real name. She rounded up bulls that couldn't stop talking because they couldn't end a sentence, and then cut them off with the right punctuation.

"It's a bigger problem than you'd think," Punk said. "Some of the bulls out there haven't stopped talking for years. They've lost track of what they were saying, so they're confused. Most of their friends have stopped listening to them completely, so, as you can imagine, they're also lonely and pretty cranky."

"Kahiko sent us," Eddie said. "We're here for the box."

Punk nodded. She closed the corral and told the others to follow her. She led the group to a little brown barn. "I used to hang with Kahiko, so when I trapped this varmint in my hayloft, I knew it had to be one of his."

In a corner of the barn, behind a stack of hay bales, there was a wire cage. Inside the wire cage was a shiny black box with deep gold accents. The box made little clicking noises with its teeth.

"It's so pretty," said Emma. "Can I be the handler this time?"

That was fine with Kim and Eddie. Uncle and Punk wished them luck and left the barn to give them privacy. Emma put the box on the hay-covered floor in front of her, and Eddie and Kim joined her in their makeshift circle. When they all felt ready, Emma put her hands on the magical box.

"Box, I wish to open your locks," Emma said. "I can answer your riddle, I'm crazy like a fox."

Then, in a small sweet voice, the box gave them this riddle:

I can take you to a place that isn't real,
Or in a restaurant, get you a meal.
I can tell you a company's numbers,
Or hold a hotel room for your slumbers.
If I'm thrown at you, you gotta be bad,
But if you're on my good side, I'll never be mad. †

Emma couldn't even begin to imagine what the riddle was talking about. She glanced down at the letter lei for help. "I think I'm going to be sick," it spelled out, and then promptly pretended to be asleep.

Kim slowly repeated the riddle in her head. She'd have to be super patient thinking about this one. First, she would look for the connections in the contradictions. She couldn't help but feel sorry for Eddie. Word games weren't his thing, and this one was a doozy.

Instead, Eddie couldn't believe how connected everything was in his life. Maybe it was always like this and he just never saw it before. Or maybe it was only here on this magic island — but he didn't think so. For one thing, Kumu told him this answer before he ever heard of Aloha Island. Excitement ran through him. Eddie saw himself in Kumu's store, positive that whatever Kumu said was useless. Useless? Kumu had only completely saved the day. And Eddie burst out laughing at the total craziness of it.

"Book!" Eddie said through his laughter. "It's book! Go ahead, say the words and tell that toothy little monster."

"Cut it out, Eddie," Kim said. "We have to stay focused and work together."

"The answer is 'a book,' Kim," Eddie said. "Believe me." And he explained Kumu's joke that was just like this riddle. "A book takes you places in your imagination," he said. "You book a table in a restaurant. A company's numbers are in its books. You book a hotel reservation. When a judge gives people a stiff sentence it's called 'throwing the book' at them."

Kim and Emma beamed at Eddie, and he knew he'd remember how they were looking at him for the rest of his life. Then Emma gave the answer to the box. A short time later, the three of them spilled out of the barn whooping and laughing, and ran over to Uncle with the second piece of the Explore Stone.

Uncle looked at the stone piece closely and grinned again. It was the second piece. All they needed was the crowning piece with the open eye carved in it. Then they could plant the stone again near Aunty's house and Aloha Island would be safe from Ignorance forever.

That night, excitement and pride washed over Eddie and kept him awake. He got up and walked to a rise that looked out over the slope of the volcano. The moon was full and he could see all the way down to the silver light shining on the distant water.

He played that look from Emma and Kim over and over again in his head. These were word puzzles and he'd been right, not once, but twice. Sure, Emma got the first one at almost the same time he did, but he'd said it first. It was the kind of school stuff that always made him look like a doofus, and he'd gotten the answer first, before Kim, even. This was amazing.

He couldn't wait until they found the next box. He knew he'd ace the answer to its riddle, too, and he'd be three for three. Kim didn't get it. It was easy for her to say it wasn't about winning when she'd always be better at reading and writing than he'd ever be.

Now she'd see Eddie Akamai standing in the winner's circle this time—just him—not Kim Kokua, and not anyone else. He was ready to sweep tomorrow; look out for number one and the rest would take care of itself. He was pumped.

Chapter 35

The Darkest Hour

The Explorer bumped down the road toward the Lying Strait. Kim and Eddie walked in front as usual, with Batbat flying ahead. Uncle drove the Explorer with Emma and the letter lei beside him. Charley Crab and Pinky the Nene spent the day arguing about which of them was more ridiculous.

Uncle didn't like that they were getting so close to the Lying Strait. The sky was grayer and darker over there, so close to the Dark Atoll and its vapors. He had heard from Biggie Large, the humpback whale who had been in that area of the Lying Strait, that Awful Lies, the invasive seaweed spreading from the Dark Atoll, had completely covered the seabed there and poisoned the water.

"There are so many lies floating around up there, the fish can't breathe," Biggie had said. Biggie also saw drift nets strung across the Lying Strait from the Dark Atoll. The Ignorance gang was catching underwater letters drifting from Aloha Island. But the nets caught dolphins, seals, and turtles, too.

Batbat broke Uncle's contemplation when he circled the Explorer and squeaked, "Target found!"

Batbat landed next to Emma. Everyone else in the Explorer had fallen asleep. Uncle was about to ask Batbat why he wasn't tired, when he noticed he couldn't see Batbat's face. Batbat was wearing a tiny gas mask.

Chapter 36

The Worst Possible Thing

Eddie and Kim trudged on, looking for any sign of a cove where they might find the third box. Eddie glanced back and saw that Batbat, with something weird covering his head, was talking to Uncle as the Explorer clunked along behind them. As he turned back around, Eddie felt dizzy, and he realized he was tired, more tired than he'd felt in a long time. He turned to Kim and saw that she was resting on a fallen log by the side of the trail.

"Just for a minute," she said. "I'm so sleeeepy..." And she leaned over and dozed off.

Eddie saw that the fallen log was at the entrance to a small cave. Next to the cave was an old wooden sign. The sign looked like this:

PIRUTS KOVE – DONUT DISTRB

"Kim! Kim!" Eddie cried, suddenly exploding with energy. He knew they had found where the third box might be hidden, and he shook all the dizziness and tiredness off him like a dog shaking off bath water. Excitement, fueled by all he felt he had to prove to himself and everybody else in the world, shot through him like an electric charge.

"It's the vapors that have her, Eddie," Uncle said, as he walked up behind them. They got Kim to her feet and walked her around to wake her up. "It smells like Apathy's work. Everyone's fighting exhaustion except Batbat with his gas mask." Then Uncle noticed how energized and focused Eddie was. "Aren't you tired, Eddie?"

"Not now I'm not," Eddie said. "I'm all set to find the third box. I know I can solve the riddle."

Eddie realized the box could be in the cave, right in front of them. With a little effort, he and Uncle got both Kim and Emma awake enough to function, and then Eddie stepped toward the entrance of the cave.

"Come on," he said. "Follow me."

Uncle, Emma, and Kim followed Eddie into the dark cave. Water dripped from the ceiling of the cave as they walked farther and farther into the darkness.

"Eeew, gross!" Emma yelped, as she brushed the slick, moss-covered wall side of the cave. Then she ran to grab Kim's hand.

"Shhh," Eddie whispered, "I hear something."

Then they all heard it—dark, deep mumbling, grumbling, and growling—like the cave itself was angry about them being there. They turned a corner and stepped into a room filled with a shimmering gold light. Eddie, Uncle, Kim, and Emma stopped in their tracks and stared.

Treasure chests overflowing with bright, shining golden *R*'s lined the walls. More chests stuffed with vowels in every color of the rainbow covered the floor. But what the group was staring at were the three dirty brown lumps in the middle of the room. The biggest lump was in the middle, with a skinny lump on one side and a short lump on the other.

"Arrgh, landlubbers!" said the short brown lump.

"The lumps are the pirates!" Emma yelled.

Reading each other's minds, Kim and Eddie immediately split up. As Eddie snooped around the cave looking for the magic box, Kim, with Uncle and Emma, stepped up to distract the pirates.

She said, "We don't want to disturb you—"

"Be gone, bilge rats!" said the big dirty pirate in the middle, laying his hand on a nasty-looking saber. "Did ye not see our sign?"

"I did," Kim said, "and I'd like to buy a dozen glazed donuts."

Emma snickered at Kim's joke. She, too, had seen the pirates' misspelled sign when Eddie and Uncle woke her up.

"Do we look like wee bakers to you? This is Pirates' Cove! We are pirates and buccaneers with short tempers and long swords—so be gone, before one of us runs you through. We be frustrated!"

From out of the corner of her eye, Kim could see Eddie going back farther into the dark corners of the cave, looking for the magic box.

"Do as he said, leave us, perky-smirk! It be frustratin' mysteries we be trying to solve!" said the skinny pirate.

Kim had to figure out some way to keep them occupied until Eddie could get out. Just then, the short pirate hit a vowel chest with his spyglass and an *i* floated into the air. The skinny pirate hit a gold treasure chest and an *r* floated up behind the *i*, and they floated together above the pirates' heads like this – **ir**.

"Arrr," said the big pirate. And the **ir** deflated and fell to the floor with a *plop*.

"*Arrrgh!*" yelled the big pirate, totally out of patience.

And then Kim knew how to calm the pirates and keep them occupied. "*R*-controlled vowels bothering you?" she asked, stepping closer to the pirates.

"Aye, lass, that's what they be called. You know of these monsters?"

Kim sure did. "In a word, when a vowel is followed by an *r* it makes a special sound," she said. "So it's called an *r*-controlled vowel."

Then she showed the pirates the right sounds for the *r*-controlled vowels, and gave them words for examples: y**ar**d, t**er**m, b**ir**d, st**or**m, and n**ur**se. Then, as Kim worked with each of the pirates—Ahoy (big), Matey (short), and Avast (skinny)—on their pronunciation, Eddie bounded out of the back of the cave with the last magic box. At first the pirates were suspicious, until they saw the box.

"You can have that useless thing," said Ahoy. "We thought it might have *r*'s inside, but it bit Matey when we tried to open it."

Everybody ended up happy. The kids and Uncle left with the magical box. The pirates were left with new knowledge they were going to put into practice as soon as they took a nap. By the time Uncle and the kids got up to the meadow where the Explorer was parked, Eddie was nearly jumping out of his skin with anticipation.

"Let's get going," Eddie said to Kim and Emma. "It's my turn to be the handler. Why don't we do it over there, under that mango tree?"

Uncle thought it might be wise to get farther away from this area and its vapors before the kids tried to solve the riddle. But Eddie didn't want to wait, and the girls seemed to be feeling better, so away they went to the mango tree with the magical box.

Under the mango tree, Eddie sat with his hands on the box in front of him and said, "Box, I wish to open your locks, I can answer your riddle, I'm crazy like a fox."

The box, this one a gleaming red that made it look like a big piece of cherry candy, spoke this riddle in an innocent, young voice:

> *We are little creatures;*
> *All of us have different features.*
> *One of us in glass is set;*
> *One of us you'll find in jet.*
> *Another you may see in tin,*
> *And number four is boxed within.*
> *If the fifth you should pursue,*
> *It can never fly from you.*
> *What are we?*†

At first, Eddie's mind reacted like it used to and froze in panic. This riddle made absolutely no sense. Pursue a fly? In a jet? No, he was getting it mixed up. He started from the top of the riddle, repeating it in his head. It would come to him. It did the other times.

Emma had been feeling wide-awake until she sat down. She'd had a nap in the Explorer, but now was suddenly was so tired that she couldn't keep her eyes open. She didn't understand the riddle, but it was the nicest-sounding one so far. Little creatures…like on Aloha Island…creatures and letters… Wait, letters? Maybe the answer was in the letters. It could be… But before she could finish her thought, she was asleep.

Kim liked this riddle. There was a pattern in it. If they talked it through, she was sure some simple and logical thinking would reveal the answer. If she could only stop yawning.

"Eddie," she said, stifling another yawn, "I see a pattern, don't you? It's like the meaning of the words doesn't matter somehow." Kim stopped for a huge yawn.

I'll have to do this myself, Eddie thought. That was OK, it's what he wanted anyway. He'd already proved he was as good at word games as he was at catching fish. Fish. That was it. Fish.

It came out of the blue, just like the other answers. But what was it that Kim had said — something like the meaning of the words didn't matter? No, my idea's right: fish. And it fits — "little creatures, different features, in glass" — an aquarium maybe. OK, tropical fish. Jet is another word for black, plenty of black fish, and sardines are in a tin —

"Eddie," Kim said, trying to rouse herself, "I'm sorry I'm suddenly so tired. Let's talk about the puzzle. It has something to do with the letters in the words."

"It's all right, Kim. I've got it," Eddie said. "It's fish."

"What?" said Kim.

"Sardines are in a tin, fish are shipped in boxes a lot, flying fish don't really fly —"

"No, wait. That can't be it," Kim said.

"That's what you said about book," Eddie said. "You just can't accept that I'm better at this than you. I'm a good guesser."

That sounded so wrong coming out of his mouth that Eddie couldn't believe he actually said it. It didn't matter; he couldn't waste time second-guessing himself. If he wanted to solve the third riddle he had to go for it. So what if it was the first answer that popped into his head? The other ones were too, weren't they? He couldn't remember exactly, maybe they weren't. It didn't matter anyway—he was going for it. Champ guesser and hero, in one move. Not bad, yeah?

"Box," Eddie said, "we have the key."

"Then please give it to me," said the box, as sweetly as the other boxes had.

"Fish," Eddie said.

For a second, nothing happened. Eddie looked down at the box's mouth, expecting the last stone piece to be presented to him.

But what came out of the box's mouth was a whimpered little word: "No." The air filled with thin smoke, and with a loud *bang* the box crushed itself down to the size of a kukui nut.

The noise woke Emma, who sat up with a start and, not knowing what had happened, smiled and said, "Vowels! The answer to the riddle is the vowels *a, e, i, o, u.*" Kim put her arm around Emma.

No, this can't be, thought Eddie. He stared at the small round black thing that used to be the box. This can't be real. This can't be real. I didn't…I couldn't have done this.

Ignorance's laughter rolled across the night sky from the Dark Atoll and told Eddie that he had. And then, for the first time since his father died, Eddie cried.

Chapter 37

Where's Eddie?

Aunty Pono marched down the road toward the cove. She heard Ignorance's laugh echoing across the Lying Strait, and she realized what must have happened. She walked faster, because she knew Ignorance had already made his first move. Aunty Pono came around a bend in the road and saw the Explorer parked near a mango tree. She broke into a run. She had to get to the kids. If she could keep the kids together, they still might have a chance.

Everybody around the Explorer was in the middle of reacting to the disaster of Eddie's wrong answer to the riddle. They all agreed that Emma had been right, but that what happened wasn't Eddie's fault, really. As Kim was comforting Emma, Uncle was kneeling at the back of the Explorer trying to cheer up the morose, frightened creatures, so no one noticed when Aunty ran up. And immediately, Aunty realized there was something else they hadn't noticed.

"Where's Eddie?" Aunty said.

****

Eddie was standing on the edge of a cliff. A very high, steep cliff. He wasn't thinking of jumping or anything. He was just cried out and numb, and he'd come up here to maybe get a different view on things. But up here or down there—it was all the same. It was like he had always expected; the moment of truth arrived, and he came up empty. Only it was worse now, Eddie thought, because this time he had been deluded enough to actually believe in himself.

He looked down at the charred round remains of the box and the piece of stone that could have saved the day. Now it looked like nothing more than a lump of charcoal. He thought about tossing it into the water, but decided to take it home and put it in his room to remind him what a loser he was — if he ever got home.

Eddie had no idea what he'd do next, but he sure didn't think he'd be too welcome around Uncle and Aunty. He put the charred thing in his pocket. He turned back toward the path, only to find Peka staring him in the face.

"Hey, slick, why so down in the mouth?" Peka said.

"Come on, Peka," said Eddie. "Can't you leave me alone? You guys are going to win. I blew it."

"Wait," Peka said. "You think that menehune box trick is permanent?"

"Yeah," said Eddie, "because it is."

As they walked on, Peka began planting her seeds of hope. But it was a Dark Atoll kind of hope. It was hope for a do-over, hope that there was a back door you could walk through and things would return to the way they had been. Peka's seeds of hope weren't actually hope at all. They were lies. But by the time the pair were at the base of the cliff, they had grown into a new reality for Eddie.

It was all magic, Peka said, and magic was rigged. Peka knew for a fact that the last piece of stone had been switched out. Ignorance had it. If Eddie would meet with him, he'd see that

Ignorance didn't want war. It was too much for him to handle; because obviously, Ignorance was ignorant. Duh, right?

Eddie felt himself being persuaded to go make a deal with Ignorance himself. It felt nice. It felt easy. And it felt just plain perfect as he walked across the Lying Straight on the thick mounds of Awful Lies seaweed and took his first steps on the Dark Atoll.

****

Back at the Explorer, Aunty Pono was in battle mode. She already had Batbat scouring the area for Eddie and had everybody else getting ready to go. "We have very little time," she explained. "The attack has already begun. Box jellies are clogging our beaches, and Ignorance's air and ground forces are poised to strike. We have to get back to the house to defend Aloha Island."

"What about my brother?" asked Emma.

Just then, Batbat landed next to Emma, out of breath. "I saw him," he said. "The Flaming Illiterates are taking him to the Dark Atoll."

"We have to save him!" cried Emma.

"We will, don't worry," said Kim.

"Right! Let's go!" said Charley Crab.

Aunty and Uncle Aka shared a look. Uncle said, "If we do that—"

"We'll be captured, just like Eddie," Aunty finished. "We have to get back and counterattack Ignorance with all our forces."

"No! We can't leave without Eddie," said Kim.

"Kim, Emma, listen to me," Aunty said. "The *only* way to get Eddie back is for us to return to headquarters and win the War of the Words. We can still do it without the Explore Stone. But we can't do it unless we keep focused and stay together."

Worried, but determined, the group headed back, with Kim and Emma worried about Eddie most of all. But as Batbat flew recon, he couldn't shake the vision he couldn't tell anyone about, especially Kim and Emma. Eddie didn't look like a prisoner when Batbat saw him. He looked like he was joining them. Once again, just like when Kahiko saw Eddie talking to Peka at Prime Minister Rule's, it looked like Eddie was a traitor.

Chapter 38

War of the Words Part 1: Ignorance in Charge

Eddie followed Peka and the Flaming Illiterates as they led him toward the crumbling shadowy volcano where Ignorance himself waited for Eddie, deep inside Ignorance Cave. Eddie still held on to the lies Peka had strung out to lure him onto the Dark Atoll, but the more he saw of this place, the harder it was to hold on to them.

The sky was even thicker with swirling, dark gray clouds than it had been over Pirates' Cove. When they had crossed the reef and stepped through the shallow lagoon, they were swallowed by a sticky, foul-smelling mist. As Eddie squinted, trying to see where to step on the swampy ground, hundreds of silent, empty-eyed, transparent people floated up around him. Eddie jumped back, but he was surrounded.

"Hey! Get away from me!"

They didn't move, they just stared at him with nothing in their eyes—nothing at all. They were so nothing from head to toe that Eddie could literally see right through them. The Flaming Illiterates burst out laughing as Eddie shivered with revulsion.

"We call that Loser Lagoon," Peka said. "Those bozos fought back after Ignorance first liberated the place. A man gives you freedom from words, and you try an overthrow? That's what you get. Ghost Town's up ahead. You'll like that better."

Ghost Town was another joke name from Peka and the Flaming Illiterates, and Eddie didn't like the place any better at all. There were many more people and creatures, though, and at least they weren't transparent. They walked around doing ordinary things like growing letters and trimming back trees, but the letters were all gray and the people had the same awful fake smile, and none of them said a thing.

"They're just as empty as the see-through bunch," Peka said. "Ignorance thought they should look happy, so he gave them smiles." That got snickers from the pig and the cockroach.

On the edge of Ghost Town, in a split second when he wasn't being watched, a beautiful woman dressed in gray like the others brushed by Eddie. Then she was gone. She looked very familiar, but Eddie couldn't see how that was possible. A few steps farther and she was walking straight at him and staring into his eyes. Her eyes weren't empty—they were filled with a frightening fire. She pushed Peka out of the way and was only an inch from Eddie's face when she turned away.

"That Mill Witch is a major pain," grumbled Peka.

"Yeah, why don't Ignorance lock her up or something?" asked the cockroach.

"Ask him yourself, smart-aleck," Peka said, as they stopped in front of the foul-smelling hole that was the entrance of Ignorance Cave.

Eddie turned back to watch the Mill Witch, who drifted away from them, but held his eyes until he was shoved into Ignorance Cave. Eddie lost his footing and tumbled down crude stone steps to the smoky pit where Ignorance, Fear, and Apathy waited for him on their dark thrones.

Eddie got to his feet and stood looking at the three foul beasts bent on destroying Aloha Island. All three were huge and nasty-looking, and seated on the middle throne, Ignorance was the largest and ugliest of them all. But as they cackled and snickered at him, Eddie couldn't help but see that behind their icky, scary appearance, how frightened and, well, dull they all looked.

"The stone is a burnt, powerless piece of nothing!" cackled Fear. "It's gone forever and you did it, just like that worthless little menehune said you would!"

It broke Eddie's heart that his pride and stubbornness had allowed these three sickos to win. Tears of frustration welled in his eyes as he thought that somehow, some way, even at this late hour, he had to find a way to stop them.

The three ghouls misread Eddie's tears, of course. "Aw, does that make you cry, Eddie Akamai?" sneered Apathy. "What's the matter, you don't like to lose, loser?"

Despite everything that had happened, and in spite of how disappointed he was with himself, Eddie held his head high in front of this bunch and he faced them head-on.

"You are very selfish, and you have lost, Eddie Akamai," said Ignorance. "You have lost and you have disappeared, just like the stone. You have disappeared from your sister's heart, and from your friend Kim's heart as well. Your failure is one thing. But the little bat saw you walk over to us. We watched as he flitted back to

Aunty Pono. *Traitor* is a word they love to throw around over there, isn't it? And it fits you so well." The three of them cackled happily.

"But don't worry," said Apathy, "you'll see your loved ones soon enough—in Ghost Town!" And they laughed again like spoiled kids in a vat of ice cream.

"Go," Ignorance thundered. "We're done with you. Now we destroy Aloha Island."

Without saying a word to them, Eddie turned his back and walked up the stone steps and out of the cave.

Peka and the rest of the Flaming Illiterates were disappointed they didn't get a promotion for dragging Eddie over to the Dark Atoll. But, if the big guys didn't want anything to do with Eddie Akamai, neither did the Flaming Illiterates. Besides, they had to get fitted for their cool new battle helmets and spears. So they walked off and left Eddie alone in the middle of the Dark Atoll.

Eddie stood there, determined to stop all this, but at the same time unable to see a way to do it, or anything, after the mess he'd made. *But wait – Peka called that ghost with the eyes the Mill Witch. Witches could do spells, and magic, right? And the Flaming Illiterates didn't like her, so that had to mean something. Witch…where would she be? Maybe there's a mill around here, which would make sense.*

Eddie looked around for a mill, but honestly he wasn't sure what to look for; he'd only seen pictures of them in history books. He finally found what he thought must have been a mill before it started crumbling to the ground, but he wasn't sure, until the beautiful witch woman stepped out of the shadows. Her eyes still held that fire.

"Looking for the Mill Witch?" she said.

Eddie nodded, not sure what to say. The witch smiled a real smile and held out her hand in greeting.

"I am Kanoa, a close friend of Aunty Pono's and Uncle Aka's," she said. "You must be the famous Eddie Akamai."

Chapter 39

War of the Words Part 2: The Amazing Eddie

Aunty and Uncle's place, otherwise known as HQ, was a beehive of activity as creatures, kids, Aunty Pono, and Uncle Aka prepared for the battle of their lifetime. And also, as a matter of fact, there were lots of spelling bees there, too. Aunty had recruited them for the air force to fight the Ignorance mosquito squadrons.

Aunty Pono knew Ignorance would order the mosquitoes to strike at the letters and words on Aloha Island first. If Ignorance could destroy the letters and words, ideas and hope would have nowhere to grow, and in a snap their Thinking Army would fall flat and Ignorance would have his victory. So Aunty put Charley Crab in charge of Word Defense. Words and letters were being hidden under eaves, behind hedges, under tarps, and tucked in burrows and nests — anywhere and everywhere that could give them cover.

Biggie Large was right offshore directing sea operations as guest admiral. Over in what used to be the letter garden, Uncle showed Aunty Pono the Word Bomb Cannon he'd made by reversing the polarity on the dark energy he had gotten from Ignorance.

"It's pretty simple when you think about it, Aunty," Uncle said. "If Ignorance uses dark energy to strip away meaning, then reversing that energy will *provide* meaning."

Just then, Batbat zoomed low overhead and screeched at the top of his voice, "The invasion is on! Ignorance is coming!" And boy, was it ever. Squadrons upon squadrons of mosquitoes flew over, intent on sucking thoughts and passion from anything they could find.

They went after all the fun, delicious words and phrases because Ignorance, Fear, and Apathy especially hated words that made people happy and feel good about themselves. First to get hit were *Hot Pink, Surf 'n' Turf, Weekend, No Homework Tonight,* and *Cookies 'n' Cream.* Charley Crab was beside himself. He had these guys well hidden, but they just wouldn't stay still. Try to keep *Hot Pink* and *No Homework* under wraps.

The mosquitoes were so fast that the spelling bees couldn't stop them from hitting their targets. The bees came back to the landing field discouraged and exhausted.

Out in the ocean, armies of sea jellies washed over the reef, and no amount of tail smacking by the twin dolphins, Jay and Kay, could swat them away fast enough. The jellies kept coming and coming in wave after wave. Every creature they stung was instantly empty and sucked across the Lying Straight to the dead lagoons of the Dark Atoll. Jay and Kay's friends the sea turtles had said they'd help, but were nowhere to be found. The Great Ignorance Jellyfish Attack appeared unstoppable.

Emma was down at one of the tide pools trying to hide *Lemonade* and *Let Me Help You with That* in the shallow water, when Biggie's voice boomed across Aloha Island. "Emma Akamai! We need your song!"

Emma nearly jumped out of her skin. What a crazy idea. How could her song help? But Ollie the Octopus thought it was a good idea, and he convinced her to strap a bucket filled with seawater over her shoulder for him to float in and be her drummer when they marched around HQ. And anyway, when Biggie called, what was a girl to do?

So there she was, standing by the bumblebee airstrip with an octopus in a bucket around her neck and mosquitoes attacking every letter and word they could find, when Ollie started drumming that reggae rhythm on the side of the bucket. Emma took a big breath and began to sing.

> *Hear my alphabet, sister sun*
> *Hear my alphabet, brother moon*
> *A - B - C - D - E - F - G*
> *I sing it for you, I sing it for me*
> *H - I - J - K - L - M - N - O - P*
> *I sing it high up in a tree*
> *Q - R - S - T - U - V - W*
> *I sing it for me, I sing it for you*
> *X - Y - Z*
> *I sing it down below the sea*

Emma sang as loud as she could, and marched all over the place and banged on her bucket. What a difference! Creatures sang along and smiled again.

With Emma's song inspiring everyone, Aunty sent the bees back into the fight. They got in formation to meet the second wave. They found their rhythm and sprayed the mosquitoes well before they could find their targets. The spray made the mosquito squadrons fall right out of the sky. The little pests suddenly had to deal with layers of meaning they had never experienced before, and they couldn't remember how to fly or why they'd even want to. Instead, they quit the fight in droves and walked off, looking at the ground and at each other's wings and going, "Hmmm."

Emma's song could even be heard out in the ocean, where Jay and Kay were nearly surrounded by jellyfish and about to give up hope, when a triggerfish sentry yelled out "Sea turtles! And...and a whole lot of...I don't know *what* those things are."

It turned out "those things" were sunfish. The sea turtles guiding the sunfish had gotten lost on the way, but Emma's song had brought them home. And the sunfish were huge—huger than huge. They looked like enormous fat plates, and as odd-looking as they were, they had always had a special place in their hearts for Uncle Aka and Aloha Island. They picked up the reading bug there, when Uncle nursed one of them back to health after he was run over by a freighter. Reading comes in handy when you're a sunfish floating around in the ocean for years and years at a time.

The other reason the sunfish showed up, besides being loyal friends to Uncle and Aloha Island, was that, like the sea turtles, they loved to eat jellyfish. And when there were so many guys that big in one place that loved to eat jellyfish, the jellyfish in that place were in trouble. The sea turtles and sunfish hit the reef like it was a no-pay drive-through and the Ignorance jellyfish were nothing but lunch.

But then, as another wave of jellyfish approached the beach, and more mosquitoes swarmed out of the swamps, Ignorance released his hordes of cockroach shock troops. Hundreds of thousands of cockroaches were on the march, tromping across Aloha Island toward Aunty's HQ and searching for frightened words and letters to devour. Uncle manned his Word Bomb Cannon and let fly with stronger words. He knew that words fortified with meaning and purpose could work miracles, and boy, they needed a miracle now.

Cockroaches chewed up letters. Chomped on words. Destroyed phrases and ideas. Anything to bring Ignorance to Aloha Island. But suddenly they were hit with Uncle's word bombs.

Compassion exploded in the midst of a very tough-looking bunch, knocking them silly.

"Mort, how are you anyway? How're the kids?" said one cockroach. "Good, good," Mort replied. "And what a nice day it is."

That happened all over the battlefield. Similar results were recorded for *empathy*, *tolerance*, and *forgiveness*. But there were so many cockroaches, so many mosquitos, so many jellyfish, and they kept coming and coming. It didn't seem there could ever be enough meaningful words and loyal friends to turn the tide.

****

Back on the Dark Atoll, Eddie told Kanoa of his friendship with Kim, and his love for his sister, Emma.

"And because I am selfish, I betrayed them," he said.

"That's not true," Kanoa said. "That's Ignorance talking."

Even though she was thousands of years older than he was, Kanoa felt she and Eddie were a lot alike. She told Eddie that Ignorance was wrong, Eddie was not selfish. He was stubborn and single-minded, as she was, but that wasn't necessarily all bad. She told Eddie that she had felt responsible for the souls who had fought against Ignorance and were trapped here.

"But I didn't want help," Kanoa said. "Impatient, and afraid our prophecy was wrong, I acted alone and failed. I shamed Aka and Aunty. They will never forgive me." She smiled at Eddie. "What was your great crime, Eddie Akamai? Perhaps I can at least help you make things right."

Eddie explained what had happened to the stone, and how he let *his* pride and fear destroy it.

Kanoa looked at him. "Make a new piece," she said. "Once you accept the gifts offered by others, your strength will become real power." She picked up a stone off the ground and handed it to him. "Do you have something to draw with?" she asked.

He pulled out the charred round thing that used to be the magic box. Then she told him what to do. With the charred stone, Eddie drew the Explore eye on a new stone. He looked up at Kanoa, then back at the stone. It glowed. It was hot in Eddie's hand. The drawing of the eye burned deep into its surface.

"Now run," said Kanoa. "Put it with the other pieces. Go!"

But Eddie stopped and turned back to Kanoa. "Uncle Aka loves you, you know," he said. "So does Aunty Pono."

Kanoa shook her head. "I can never go back."

"Accept the gifts of others, remember?" Eddie said. "They're your family!"

Kanoa couldn't believe what she was about to do. "OK," she said, "I'll go with you, but you must deliver the stone. No matter what, you keep going."

Eddie nodded. "You ready?" he asked.

They ran across the spongy seaweed still clogging the Lying Straight. They hit the sand of Aloha Island, and ran harder. Behind Eddie and Kanoa, Ignorance, Apathy, and Fear roared in white-hot fury.

As Eddie and Kanoa raced across the sand, Ignorance rose in terrible black clouds behind them. Eddie kept his grip tight on the piece of stone, and kept his head down and his stride steady. He knew he'd make it because of Kanoa's words: "If you accept the gifts of others, your strength will become real power."

Ignorance threw lightning first, melting the sand and turning it to glass at their feet, but Kanoa saw it coming and helped Eddie jump clear. Then a huge boulder came crashing out of the sky, and Eddie pushed Kanoa out of the way just in time. More lightning, and they kept jumping clear; more boulders, and they kept dodging them. The three dark spirits screamed and howled in frustration. This could not be! He was only a boy!

By the time Eddie and Kanoa closed in on the Old Stones Place, the sky was filled with so many boulders and so much lightning that it was like a hailstorm for giants. Following the frantic Batbat, Eddie ran right to the Old Stones Place, where Kim and Emma were waiting for him.

Chapter 40

Three Heroes

Eddie was so glad to see Emma and Kim, and they were so glad to see him, that all they wanted to do was throw their arms around each other and hug themselves silly. But when Eddie held up the new Explore capstone, they knew that some very important business had to come first.

With fighting and explosions going on all around them, Eddie put Emma's hands and Kim's hands on the stone, so that all three of them were holding it at once.

"It's the only way it will work," Eddie said. "It's the only way it would ever work. We have to do this together."

So Eddie, Kim, and Emma—all three together—put the capstone on the other two pieces, and in a blinding flash the Explore Stone glowed as one. Then, Aunty Pono, Uncle Aka, and Kanoa stepped forward and joined hands in a circle with the three kids. And at that moment, there was a deafening, horrible cry of pain from Ignorance, Fear, and Apathy. They shrieked and howled as they sank into the ocean, but not before vowing to return again one day and get their revenge.

With the sound of a sweet open chord that seemed to come right out of the air, all the fighting stopped, the Awful Lies seaweed began melting away, the sun cracked through the clouds, the gray sky turned to blue, the ghosts and transparent people found that they were filling with life and color, and slowly, elegantly, the Dark Atoll rose from the sea and became Mele Island again.

Once more music played in the wind, and the air between Aloha Island and Mele Island was filled with ideas and dreams. And best of all, bright colorful letters and words grew everywhere you looked.

And what a celebration everybody had that night. Creatures were singing and dancing and letters were flying through the air. Kanoa and Uncle Aka danced in the moonlight as Aunty Pono stirred up the most wonderful stew anyone had ever tasted. Even the pirates showed up with chests of golden *R*'s. But Aunty Pono could tell that the guests of honor at the luau weren't as happy as everyone else. She knew that even heroes get homesick. It was time for Aunty Pono to work some serious magic again and send Eddie, Kim, and Emma back to Honolulu.

Aunty Pono not only made sure that the children got back home safely, and that they got to school on time that day, because on Oahu no time had passed. Home was just as they had left it, but it felt brand-new to all three of them.

Surprising everyone except Kim and Emma, Eddie signed up for tutoring help from programs at his school. He also went to Kumu for reading help on weekends. When they took a break, Eddie told Kumu jaw-dropping stories of a place called Aloha Island.

Eddie gave up guessing about anything. He didn't even guess the time. If he didn't know something, he didn't pretend he did. He asked for help—like he was doing right now, with his hand raised in English class. But before the teacher could turn from the blackboard and see him, something brown and furry flew in the window and landed on Eddie's desk.

"Batbat," Eddie whispered, "what are you doing here?"

"I'm sorry to interrupt, Eddie, especially English class," Batbat said, "but we need your help. I promise it will only take a second—of your time, anyway."

Before Eddie could answer, he caught a glimpse of Kim and Emma peeking around the corner of the school and waving at him.

They were floating in a golden bubble.

About the Author

Frank South, formerly a television writer and producer, now writes stories and plays from his home in Georgia, where he lives with his family. This is his first book.

His website is www.franksouth.net.

You can find *Aloha Island* reading lesson plans for parents and teachers, as well as information about coming multimedia educational fun and games at the official website:

www.thealohaislandinc.com

Printed in Great Britain
by Amazon